THE DEPOSITION

THE DEPOSITION

PETE DUVAL

University of Massachusetts Press
Amherst and Boston

ISBN 978-1-62534-570-7 (paper)

Designed by Sally Nichols
Set in Dante Pro and Bebas Neue
Printed and bound by Books International, Inc.

Cover design by Sally Nichols
Cover art by Agnolo Bronzino, *The Deposition of Christ,* 1540–1545, oil on panel.
Wickimedia Commons, public domain.

Library of Congress Cataloging-in-Publication Data
A catalog record for this book is available from the Library of Congress.

British Library Cataloguing-in-Publication Data
A catalog record for this book is available from the British Library.

FOR MIKI

As soon as you say *Me,* a *God,* a *Nature,*
so soon you jump off from your stool
and hang from the beam. Yes, that word
is the hangman. Take God out of the dictionary,
and you would have Him in the street.

—*Herman Melville,*
letter to Nathaniel Hawthorne, 1851

CONTENTS

THE DEPOSITION

THE PHYSICS OF LARGE OBJECTS

You're awake, and your name is Norman. You say, "Hear that?" You say, "What is that?" But your wife doesn't stir. You twist larvally in the sheets and raise yourself to kneel on the pillow. You part the aluminum slats of the Venetian blinds, wince under their buckle and snap. Your eyes can feel the cold coming off the windowpanes. This makes sense to you, Norman; it's December. But what you see through those panes you don't immediately understand. Only moments before, or what seems like moments, you were weightless, falling like a moist clump of snowflake or ash through the warmer tiers of hypnagogia, a sensation that, interrupted, has left your joints with an over-oiled thickness and your perception a little downy at the edges. And you marvel now at how what you see out there seems to arrive in parts that your mind assembles in real time. You're aware of the texture of your awareness. It's like watching yourself totter along wearing a diaper in Super 8mm slow motion, in the desaturated medium of a hazardous photographic process. The burnt-dust smell of your dead father's overheated film projector comes to you, rising through layers of forgetting, warped reels turning, and you half expect to catch a whiff of bulb-softened celluloid. From some parallel cognitive track, a voice that often comments on what you, Norman, are doing at any moment, or thinking, the voiceover of your life, notes dryly that the analogue world so perfectly emblemized by that projector is really gone. Gone. But do you know what that even means? Gone where? It occurs to you that when the voice ceases its commentary, you'll be dead.

Or what has been "you."

But out there now, angled against the curb that separates your neighbor Boyd's yard from the broken asphalt of your street, the cab of a truck sits idling. All of the houses are dark. This makes sense; it's just after 3:00 a.m. You squeeze your eyes. You reach for your glasses. Yes. A tractor-trailer. An eighteen-wheeler. Its two-ply rear wheels rest in a bramble of lilacs at the edge of your yard. And reflected in the curve of the trailer's chrome tank, everything—the brambles, the streetlamp, the Dog Star in its brittle opalescence, even you yourself, Norman, if you look closely enough: the entire visual field stretches like taffy, in keeping with the principles of reflection and the limitations of the perceiving eye's—*your* eye's—point of view.

"Wake up," you say to your wife. Softly. She doesn't wake up.

A figure in a thick insulated jumpsuit of indeterminate hue—because of the color-sapping sodium streetlamp—opens the cab door and climbs in and closes the cab door with a fluidity suggesting long habit or studied nonchalance. The self-aware swag of a unionized laborer at work. However unlikely, you do not want to be seen by this person. Not an unusual urge these days, not for you, who spends so much of your time alone in the house, forcing yourself to do things that might or might not result in financial return; you would call it *work* if the word did not imply that what you do has a purpose, or at least some measure of innate meaning, which most work does, even to the uninformed eye and is, come to think of it, the very definition of *work*. A consequence of spending so much time "working out of the house," purposefully occupied or otherwise—sometimes, truth be told, just eating handfuls of sponge cake—is that you often find yourself in exactly this position, peeking out between blinds or ducking behind the lower half of the aluminum screen doorframe after spotting Boyd retrieving his mail or making a huge production of maintaining his lawn. So it is from long habit that you crouch a little, allowing the slats of the blinds to narrow. It's a wasted precaution because the figure in the cab seems wholly preoccupied.

You try one more time to rouse your wife, but she's dead to the world. It's sad, in a way, that she's always coming while you're always going. How, for instance, she'll be reading a book while you're down in the basement wet-vacuuming rainwater seepage off the cement floor with a red plastic hydrovac, a satisfying, sensually engulfing experience that she'll never know, and one that arouses in you an anxiety involving the inhalation of vapor-riding black mold spores that implant and spread along your lungs' pink tissue. Infiltration, deep and irreversible, and all the more nefarious for its domestic origins. Your wife's mouth hangs slack. She snores once, but doesn't move. Norman, you're on your own.

You rise finally and feel for your slippers, inexpensive black flats that figure significantly in a vaguely drawn scenario involving future lessons in kung fu. You find them. You slip them on. The sound that awoke you grows louder, clearly the grumbling of a diesel engine. *Diesel*. Even now the word still holds much of its original erotic appeal, though you no longer repeat it like a mantra to get to sleep. Such are the transient enthusiasms of the suburbs. The car you drove for close to four years—a champagne 1985 300D Mercedes-Benz—sits in your garage, cocooned in its own desuetude. That it was powered by perhaps the most successful diesel engine ever manufactured for a passenger vehicle was once a source of pride to you. Of a piece with the loose rattle and knock of its five pistons, and with your visceral intimations concerning the nature of existence.

The night air cold, you descend your back steps. You keep your eyes on the cab of the truck as you cut a diagonal across your driveway and across your lawn. Your lawn. Frozen now into hillocks, the hemorrhages of last summer's 10,000 mole-hours jam and jolt your ankles with each step. Like some object lesson in the perils of neglect, the moles' transformation of your lawn into green sponge cake has shaken you to your core. You've come to realize—perhaps too late—that they've been telling you something about yourself. Dispatched from Mount Olympus to deliver a message. The more you've researched the problem, the more aware you are that, like the agony of tooth decay prior to the advent of modern dental care, moles are something of a universal human pestilence, their mere mention wrapped in a nimbus of folklore and quack-remediation. Leave chewing gum at the rim of their holes (they'll eat it, experience excruciating constipation, and die of intestinal distress), flood their tunnels, buy a cat, rent a jackal. Your father-in-law—the man goes old-school, Midwest-style; having established a policy of zero tolerance, he hovers above his own lawn in the twilight with a sharp-edged spade, like some revenant from an excised chapter of Leviticus, until, at the merest premonition of subterranean stirring, he swoops down in theophanic fury to dismember those blind, flightless incubi.

You pause at the end of your lawn to ask yourself, What am I looking at? The truck's cab has been airbrushed with metallic high-gloss paint. On the door, in a nest of unintelligible script hoary with elaborate curlicues, hangs the face of a Medusa with wide eyes and smiling snake heads all a-writhe. The driver clunks the rig's transmission into reverse. You can see his hands on the wheel as he tries to angle the rear end free of your lilacs. They've become entangled in the undercarriage and are being yanked from the frozen earth at the roots.

You understand the situation now. The driver's trapped. He can't turn the rig around, and he doesn't trust himself enough—here you're speculating again—to back it straight down the hill to the highway half a mile distant. Nor is there a way forward. The driver must have veered off the interstate and borne right instead of left, chosen the road less traveled. Now he's doing time for this lark in a Dantean hallucination set on the edge of the suburbs, the stars cruel in their indifference, the split-level ranches arrayed like fossilized tortoises. A panic you can only imagine is mounting in the man's soul as he struggles with what should be dawning in him now—that he is, for all intents and purposes and in ways yet to be understood, screwed.

You wonder if they'll have to airlift the poor bastard out.

Then the driver opens the door and climbs down and stands with his hands on his hips. He hasn't noticed you yet, except he isn't a he, he's a she.

"I take it," you say, clearing your throat, "we have a problem."

The driver startles, spins. "Oh, Jesus Christ," she says, "you scared the shit out of me." In the ghostly blur of the sodium lamplight—the shadows sort of starship green but limned with orange lowlights that linger and smudge when she moves—the driver could be standing on the outer skin of an orbital platform, a refueling hub for unwomaned missions to the Oort cloud. "You gotta watch that, sneaking up on people. It's dangerous."

You feel insubstantial, constituted from the interstices of night. You're just an impulse quivering on the verge of action, ghostly yourself. "Might I be of some help?"

"Not unless you can handle an eighteen-wheeler." She draws closer, her attitude relaxing. And you realize that you're on the same side, you and this woman, both human, both cold-cocked by yet another manifestation of the cussedness of things. "I can't clear that telephone pole," she says, motioning along the length of the rig. Her double, reflected in the chrome of the trailer, motions as well but in grotesque elongation. "And I can't clear her the other way either." She points at the retaining wall your neighbor Boyd constructed last summer, ending years of exasperation over the erosion of his topsoil along a steep drop-off whenever it rained.

You lean back, angling your line of sight. You want to ask her how things could have gotten this bad. You don't.

She snorts and wipes her nose. "I almost just said *the hell with this,* and took the pole out and just drove off."

"Right," you say. "The hell with it."

She leans over to spit. She's been chewing tobacco. "I'd a been in another goddamn *state* before anyone'd be the wiser."

You imagine a gaggle of wire-bedraggled telephone poles jangling madly behind the rig as it accelerates on the interstate, the driver wailing on the horn and laughing crazily.

The wad of chaw distorting her smile, she says, "'Cept now that you seen me, I gotta kill you."

You don't know what to say.

She points at the skein of lilac brambles. "Sorry about the bushes."

To imagine this barren brush bringing forth the sweet scent that envelopes the flower in April seems, to say the least, delusional.

"Those are yours?"

"Don't give them another thought."

Beneath the insulated jumpsuit, she shrugs, its stiff hood lifting from her forehead. "Oh, well." A two-way radio in the cab squelches to life, a few syllables donald-ducking into the wastes. "I'll give it one more try." She mounts the wheel guard. "Maybe you can help me, be my eyes." She jabs her crooked index and middle fingers at her own eyes, then at yours, a gesture you've always appreciated for its succinct expression of confidence and wordless camaraderie. She's wearing yellow leather gloves a cowhand might sport; they have yellow rawhide cinch-straps with little red balls at the ends. "Out back." She motions behind her. "Let me know how close I am. Can you do that for me?"

To be of service, yes. That you might begin again, the slate still damp. Might the revelation that you were once a joyful child, a proactive, barely containable force for jellybean humanism and insouciant goodness, meet with disbelief? But there's no time for looking backward. You aren't dead yet, Norman. Isn't that right?

"I'd be happy to," you say.

She smiles—you think she does—and sinks into the darkness of the cab and shuts the door, her elbow draped over the lowered window. The diesel revs, lifting tenderly the rain cap from the crown of the vertical exhaust pipe. You step into the street and draw a bead once more on the line of the trailer's rear tires—forward and back. She has room. You hear the gears shift, followed by a new and more determined engine pitch. *Blessed be thy diesel.* The wheels begin to move toward you, the rubber of the tires morphing to swallow the last of the curb like sluggish black cream. You can see the driver's face in the rectangular mirror on the near side of the cab. You wave her back, back, the distance narrowing between the pole and its chubby reflection in the curve of the chrome. What's she hauling? Butane? Liquid nitrogen? Milk? From the undercarriage, your lilacs dangle like snagged tumbleweeds.

"More, more," you tell the night. "You got it. Keep coming." She can't hear you. You indicate she should slow, your palms down as though to say, *Quiet, it's late.* She knows exactly what you mean. You stride to the open window of the cab, and she squints down at you, her jaw working. Though her face is in shadow, her breath curls wraithlike through the wash of orange lamplight. How old she is you can't say. Nor whether she might be considered attractive or not. You're beyond such conventional preoccupations. Beyond all that. Your extremities are numb. "If you cut back right just a bit," you say, "I think you can clear the pole. It won't be by much. I'm going to stand right there—" You point to a spot a few feet beyond the telephone pole, its rough surface pocked from years of abuse beneath the linesmen's climbing spurs.

She tilts her head. "I got room? You sure?"

You nod.

"How much?"

You hold your index fingers four inches apart. "Enough."

"That's not much."

"You don't need much."

Her lips tighten. "I'll tell you what, buddy, I appreciate it, but it's gonna suck if the pole comes down. Know what I'm saying?"

"The pole's not coming down. Push straight back. Then cut it right on my signal. Easy."

She sits staring straight ahead. "I think I'm going to call in, have them run someone up here who can drive."

You ride the pause for all it's worth. Then: "How long have you been hauling the big rigs?"

"A month."

You keep your face stiff. "Hell, you can do this." Look at you, Norman, impersonating a guy who knows what he's talking about, pumped tight with a bravado born of intimate familiarity with the physics of large objects—the métier of tugboat captains, crane operators, men who labor at the nation's ports of entry, durable goods and Pez dispensers by the millions in orange shipping containers stark against blue skies. The tonnage moving with the fluency of thought. You smile. You know the score. You're nobody's fool. You give her the thumbs-up, a big double heaping.

She nods, absently, her mouth bunched and bitter. She revs the engine again as you walk to your position.

In the concave surface of the tanker's rear end, as you begin to wave her on, you watch yourself. It's hard to concentrate on the task at hand. *Who is this person?* Distorted beyond recognition, bulging forward from the recesses of the night, you're a gnome with a sodium-lamp tan. But is it *you*, Norman?

As the distance between the tanker and the pole narrows to an inch, you slow her down. "Is that far enough?" Does she have enough room to clear Boyd's handsome cement-block retaining wall? Or will she carve a gash into it, and disentomb scores of frozen mole carcasses, rodent Lazari who'll wait forever for their weeping Jesus?

She thrusts her hand out the window, her forefinger and thumb indicating how much clearance is still needed up front. You wave her on, slowly. She nudges the pedal, the knobs of rubber on the rear tires creaking, creaking, until, finally, the bulge of the chrome kisses the pole.

"Hold up!" you shout. You don't move, not a muscle. The telephone and cable wires tremble above. With just your eyes you trace the faint waves of displacement that ripple outward from the pole, note their faint return. Soon the wires are still again, and you stand there wondering, were you to spread your arms and rise now into the black vault of Heaven, could they hold you down? Or would you burst through? And might you ascend into the blessed darkness to take your place, however briefly, at the right hand of the Father?

I, BUDGIE

I watch, and am as a sparrow alone upon the house top.

—Psalm 102:7

The budgie speaks of himself in the third person. This is not an affectation.

However hungry, the budgie has never eaten roadkill. Nor will the budgie, ever.

How far removed, the budgie often asks himself, is he from the feral state? And when it comes, this state, what will it look like?

On an evening much like this one, the Family left the sliding-glass doors to the deck open.

How long ago? The budgie's sense of time is unreliable. Neither watch nor calendar does the budgie own.

Supper was being served, of this the budgie is certain, the sheers billowing in with the August breeze.

Loose in the kitchen, the budgie could not resist.

Once outside, the budgie marveled at how quickly the Family

adapted to his absence, though the Blond One wept for a time while the budgie watched from atop the air conditioner that jutted from her bedroom window.

The Family finished supper: it was, and is, their practice to eat the flesh of mammals, the three of Them.

Other days They eat of the flesh of domesticated fowl. Chicken—ridiculous bird.

The budgie remembers the scent of cattle flanks sizzling in liquefied garlic.

Sometimes it was pork.

These days the budgie haunts the backyard, a specter subsisting on stale maple seeds and avoiding the shadows of hawks, resigned to his fate as a non-native species.

He would not go back; that's what the budgie tells himself.

Clinging to the fishing line with which someone—the Bald One?—has repaired the wind chimes, the budgie watches the Family as though peering into a yellowy world.

The Family in amber light.

Is the budgie lonely?

The budgie is alone.

Might it be said that the budgie embraces solitude? It might, yes.

But what of other birds? What of migratory flocks? The redbreasts of spring? The swallow and the finch?

What of the hummingbird?

The budgie would prefer not to be condescended to.

Nor to be lumped in with native species.

What of the famed parrots of Telegraph Hill? How they flourished in climes foreign and adverse? Intended by the hand of God for the tropics, they accepted their fate, unlikely immigrants making due.

Better than making due, thriving.

The budgie prefers to allow his silence at this moment to communicate all that he feels on the issue.

Today, the forecast is for storms, widely scattered. The sky to the northwest has ripened to the color of bruised plums.

Among the budgie's consolations at first was this: the Family's choice of replacement, a goldfish—now dead. It lasted two days.

The budgie watched it succumb to the rigors of careless transportation in a Ziploc bag, and to the shock of tap water.

The budgie witnessed its inglorious interment: the Blond One flushing the goldfish down the toilet.

Not that the budgie would have eaten the goldfish, if given the chance.

Today has been a particularly lean day, the budgie feeling threadbare and forlorn.

Once, the budgie could talk, but now he has forgotten the "words."

Nor would the budgie prefer to enter into a philological discussion as to whether even a single instance of the sounds he produced for choice seeds were in fact "words."

Today's a cold day for August, the sun itself a threadbare memory.

The Blond One slides open the glass door and steps forth to stand on the deck facing west, fascinated by the encroachment of the thunderhead.

Above Her the budgie lurks in the rain gutter, peering over its edge at the crown of the Blond One's head and the whirl of hair against the whiteness of Her scalp.

There was a time when the budgie would ride Her shoulder through the house, nestled into the slope of Her neck.

Does She think about the budgie now?

Before pursuing the thought any further, the budgie thinks, with a bitterness that catches him by surprise: *Spit in this hand. Wish in the other. Then check to see which one fills up faster.*

The Blond One turns, hand shading Her eyes.

The budgie squats lower in the gutter, down with the crispy maple-seed blades and the multihued grit from the tarpaper roof.

"Looks like it's going to pour," the Blond One calls into the house.

There have always been three of Them, the Family:

The Blond One, She who first retrieved the budgie from a bank of cages under fluorescent lights. A row of budgies behind smudged glass. "This one," She said, lifting him for

the Dark One, the mother, to see, who said, "Just the one?"

(From the start, the budgie couldn't keep his eyes off the Dark One.)

The Blond One nodded, turned to check among the others once more. Nodded again.

The Dark One, the older female, the mother—whenever the budgie caught glimpses of Her smooth paleness through cracks in the doors as he hung in his silvery cage, something dark would bloom in his blue-green breast.

On forays to the peak of the roof, the budgie watches for the Bald One's return, always in the cool of the evening. He's long admired the Bald One's regularity—and what the budgie has always taken for His seemingly selfless devotion to the Family.

(The budgie is quite aware of the deflationary power of clichés. But this one applies.)

Had the budgie been blessed with a mate, offspring—something he's not spent a lot of time thinking about—he could have done much worse in meeting the responsibilities resultant thereof than has the Bald One.

The Bald One's lack of affectation, His ease in His own skin, has ever impressed the budgie as well, which is why, thinking about it right now, the budgie wishes to reverse course and begin speaking in the first person.

I, budgie, do not know how much longer I have. My heart beats so fast.

(A day is as a thousand years.)

But not as fast as it beat the day I watched as the Bald One and the Dark One, in the mild afternoon of the Blond One's absence, when upon arriving home early, by intention or by luck, He from wherever He went—and still goes, I assume—in the morning, She from Her routines over the hill, lay with One Another in plain sight.

I was younger then. I rocked and bobbed in my excitement, witness to something wonderful and rare.

The Bald One lay as though skinned, white and smooth on the counterpane, the Dark One just now coming into the room.

It is said that the Lord gave dominion to Man over the animals, and who would argue with that, but sometimes the apportionment of certain anatomical specificities gives me particular pause.

I have lived among Them long enough to covet thumbs.

Back under the fluorescent lights of the pet shop, I'd watched the coupled budgies coo and preen and engage in ritual courtship.

Then as now I'd wondered why such opportunities were never afforded to me. Why was I—why am I—alone?

That day, in the room with the Bald One and the Dark One, I wanted to fly down for a closer look, to soak in the thrill of Their ardor.

For it arose, such ardor, from the nuances and particularities of order, genus, and species, I believe, into the realm of the universal;

this was the way of *all* flesh. Not just human or budgie or fish. Still, perhaps, this was something different.

I knew what was going on even though I'd not been equipped with the "words" to articulate it.

Nor did the sounds I made distract Them from the enthusiasm of Their concupiscent offices that afternoon.

And when it was over, and the Dark One lay splayed on the counterpane, the Bald One up and stirring in the rooms, I looked down upon Her with something I can only now name as tenderness.

I was not ashamed. This was more than fascination.

Budgies are nothing if not watchers, notetakers, stenographers for the End of Days.

She looked at me in my cage and smiled.

Then—I'll never get over it—by launching into the ceaseless prattle that I was ever subject to, She destroyed the moment.

The same phrase repeated *ad nauseum*. If it had been something in Latin, something less—

I choose not to remember, such was the demeaning nature of its banality.

What's that? Oh, you insist, do you? So you fancy yourself the implied addressee of a dramatic monologue?

You're absolutely right. You can't put the genie back in the bottle. You can't unlearn what you've spent so long learning.

Think you have the stomach for it, though?

Right. Here's what She said: *Wittle Wally's a big boy, yes, sir.*

I love Her anyway. As I love the Blond One, the Bald One.

Out in the green space between where I ride the crest of the roof and the distant pale blue of the western hills winds the highway, invisible but sending up its day's worth of heat.

Giving up the ghost, among other occupations of the afternoon. The dumb beautiful ministrations of the physical world.

And upon those upward rushes glide the buzzards—turkey vultures, for those with a penchant for more homey nomenclatures—whose given names I care not to learn. Given by whom? They don't have names. (Ask a blade of grass its name.)

There's no "Wally" out here, in nature.

The vultures seem more than content, happier 'n pigs in shit, to occupy that space—no more, no less—provided to them within a class of being.

Instances of *vultureness* or *vulturicity,* if you will. Devoid of identity or soul.

They constitute something of a cognate for the same space provided me in my *budgieness.*

On the updrafts see them rock like things made of starched silk.

Quite possibly, I will end up as the stuff of which they're made. You are what you eat, after all.

I suppose there are worse fates. I think of the goldfish. Poor son of a bitch.

The Family kept me in a cage with a small rectangular mirror. In it I watched myself for hours.

Watched myself right out of the slip of space provided to me in the Lord's wisdom.

Out of the ontological sentence which is "budgie."

I, having been clothed in the vestments of a proper name, fallen—or raised up?—from the syntax of the order of things.

They had intended the mirror to be a way to pass my time. A little faux companionship.

It was in the fourth millennium of my existence that I finally attributed the movements of the "budgie" in the mirror to the flit and twitter of my own will.

I de-linked the image in the mirror from the "other" I had mis-attributed it as.

Step 2: I mistook what I saw for "me." I was that shape in the mirror. I was some thing.

The edges of the self for a time clearly delineated, I took comfort in this hallucination.

But just as I awoke from the dream of the "other," so, too, did I realize that the thing in the mirror wasn't "me." God, no.

And out here even now, I can feel this awareness losing its edge within me. That's why I switched to the first person, because the third was creeping me out.

I come to in odd places—always on my feet, the echo of my name fading as in a waking dream.

Sometimes I want to deliver myself up to the maw that surrounds me, forget this fantasy of individuation. I'm an inconsequential instance of "budgie," nothing more. Anonymous despite what has been said of the sparrow's fall.

The Blond One once left the sliding-glass door open. It stood ajar in the falling light as all manner of insect made its way toward the ceiling lamp that hangs over the dinner table.

Why didn't I follow suit? I imagine the homecoming I'd have received. The Family are a gracious tribe.

But I just stood there on the deck rail, preening.

The storm is upon us, the boiling undersides of the thundercloud directly overhead.

The wind picks up, the leaves showing their own undersides.

Hopping from window to window, I anticipate a colder rush of wind. Watching.

The Dark One is nervous. She clings to bits of rubber—elastics, the sole of an old running shoe—remembering something about its nonconductive properties, no doubt.

If it comforts Her, let Her be. (Listen to the bird, speaking of condescension.)

The vultures are gone, swallowed up by the steel wool of the thundercloud.

Now the downpour: and I find my usual place to ride it out, tucked in behind one of the tin downspouts. I like to listen to the rumble of the rainwater so close.

The Blond One loves storms. She used to sit under the tree in a folding chair until the Bald One told Her the practice was unsound.

He had the stats to back it up: that 98 percent of those killed by lightning are caught sheltering under trees. And on and on.

I love storms too. Why, I don't know exactly. It has something to do with what I've been on and on about.

Something to do with the momentary feeling I get, looking up into the immensity of churning vapor as the budgie that I am seems to dissipate, not unlike the way I know my mind, my self, will dissipate someday soon.

And I realize—not just in my head but deeper, in the very budgie interstices—that this is how it should be.

It has taken me some time to realize that this budgie isn't the center of the universe.

THE DEPOSITION

It was not until V. had pulled away into the Iowa night that he noticed anything unusual: the priest he'd picked up was bleeding. Nothing dramatic, just an oozing, a glistening patch of black on black. V. decided not to mention it. For a mile or so, he didn't know what to say. The priest had a full face for a thin man, with dramatically defined tendons in his neck that seemed to tense for no particular reason, and a small, meticulously trimmed goatee, which surprised V. because he'd never known a member of the clergy to have such a goatee, not even on cable television. But he hadn't been this close to a priest for a long time.

On the way home from a deposition in Davenport, V. had taken the back roads—a whim. He didn't have many. But he'd had some time, and he'd been listening to Elvis Costello whine about how pretty words didn't mean much anymore from the digital recesses of his iPhone playlist. About half an hour into the drive he saw, from a distance, the priest—he didn't know it was a priest at that moment, not yet—leaning against a sign at the intersection of two unnamed blacktops. V. slowed the Lexus to a stop on the broken asphalt of the shoulder, and powered down the driver's-side window, and looked out at the man. Yes, it was a priest. He was dressed like one. He was standing about fifteen feet away. He wasn't carrying anything, no luggage, not even a messenger bag or a man purse (something V. knew most priests would be comfortable carrying, having long since given up on the husbandry of masculine iconographies). The man made no move, either toward or away from the car. Odd. He seemed content to return V.'s succinct acknowledgment—barely a nod—without expression. On a case years back involving gross negligence in a Church parking lot, V. had spoken over the phone a number of times with the monsignor of a parish out in Council Bluffs, a smoker, V. remembered, from the sound of his voice. The case, whose details were crushingly monotonous to stir up, had turned out badly. A mess, actually, though through no fault of V. himself. Something to file away and forget. But face to face with a man of the cloth? No. It had been decades. And the way the man just stood there. It was unnerving, and a little weird. He seemed about the same age as V., early forties, and he was dressed in black, from his patent-leather shoes, which, apart from a coating of dust, appeared to be brand new, to the all-black generic baseball cap he wore, straight-brimmed, no curve. Urban style. Maybe it was a designer Chicago Cubs hat, a black C embroidered on black canvas. Huh! Since when had baseball caps, generic, designer, urban, or otherwise, become accessories of priestly style?

"Father," V. said finally, flatly. Even now, even this early in the episode, V. had become aware of a nibbling, inchoate anxiety, as though the roused metaphysical chickens of his whimsy in taking the back roads were already making the slow turn toward home—to roost—and he felt charged by the impulse to drive away, to stomp on the gas and take immediate leave of this most disquieting dude, watch him vanish in the rearview back there with the road dust and deepening gloom. For his part, the priest seemed content simply to meet V.'s gaze with his own hooded eyes.

V. was feeling charitable. It came on him all of a sudden. "Hop in, padre." Yeah, just like that. Another whim. (They were piling up today.) This one, though—it felt like stepping into time, or history. Without batting an eye, the priest walked around, opened the passenger door, and slid efficiently inside. They pulled away.

After a few moments of silence, the man spoke first. He asked V. what he did for a living. Point blank: "What line of work you in?" He sounded a little like he was from Brooklyn, though V. had never been to New York. So he had nothing to go on but another species of mediated reductivism: "Brooklyn accent," "priest," "urban style."

V. told him the truth, that he was a lawyer.

The priest nodded and without missing a beat asked V. where he lived. He didn't seem to want the street number, just the general area. At this, V. experienced a wash of what can only be described as vertigo. (Actually, it can just as easily be described as dizziness.)

V. let loose. Come what may. "Des Moines," he said. *Bam!*

As for V.'s name, the priest didn't seem interested. Which was just as well because V. would have given him no more than an initial, even if pressed, and this most likely would have put a strain on things. And things were already strained, if for no reason other than the bleeding.

"Thanks for stopping there," the priest said after a spell. V. looked over at him. It sounded like honest gratitude, or as honest as one man can be with another in this world. He realized he was sick and tired of the uncharitable and reductive manner with which priests had been represented of late. A priest was just another guy. No big deal. It was a job. A service-economy job. That said, V. found himself visited by a tinge of annoyance. Ten minutes before, this guy, this priest, this hitchhiking priest, was walking in the near-dark along a rural highway through the middle of Iowa. And it was getting cold. The man *should* be grateful, priest or not, but then, just as fast, V. cast his mind back to what Jesus himself had to say about acts of kindness. V. forgot the exact wording. Jesus had never actually used the phrase *acts of kindness;* He hadn't even understood English. The point being, as V. recalled: not only did pride goeth before destruction, but it sucketh dry any treasures you had laid in store up in heaven. Like malpractice insurance.

Then they were miles further along and V. found himself in the middle of telling the priest all about the deposition he'd taken in Davenport, from which he was returning, and during which an overweight female client sitting across the table from him with an angelic face and mild, almost childlike, disposition, had fallen into a monumental coughing fit that V. suspected—he was sure, actually—was nothing more than an affectation, a performance, poorly executed, because the episode had lasted only long enough for each side represented in the case to agree that they could, at present, no longer continue. "Let's reschedule," said the woman's lawyer, a man V. knew only as a pair of close-knit eyes and a single eyebrow, a kind of incompetent legal cyclops of a man. As for the woman herself, she'd been doubled over, her eyes bulging. But the theatrics hadn't convinced V. Standing there holding out one of those conic paper cups of water that you have to drink from fast before they soak through, he'd felt vaguely ashamed. Even embarrassed. She should have taken the initial settlement offer he'd made. Which was ample. Years before, the woman had been injured in a traffic accident involving a reefer—trucker lingo for a refrigerated eighteen-wheeler. This one had been carrying so-called "gourmet" ice-cream sandwiches and was insured by the company V. represented. That's the kind of law V. practiced. He went to bat for insurance companies. The bigger the better. He helped minimize their exposure or, if their exposure had invited disaster and disaster had accepted the invitation, he helped minimize their damages. It was a line of work to which long ago he'd reconciled himself. Working for the Man. V. was good at what he did. He had an extensive client list. He was a rainmaker. There was no disputing this. Though no one used that phrase anymore without irony or finger quotes.

"An affectation?" the priest said. He was heaving his words a little now, bleeding as he was from the side. Surely the lungs were affected. "So you think she was faking a cough?"

V. was concerned now by what he detected as a slight *modulation* in the priest's voice, as well as an otherwise imperceptible repositioning—a stiffening?—of the man's shoulders. It was a sensitivity he'd trained himself to ignore, with considerable success, because you couldn't carry on conversations, business conversations or personal conversations, if your attention was always catching on observations of such insignificance. There just wasn't enough bandwidth for all that. Then, with a rush, V. felt afraid he'd said too much about the case; a not entirely unfounded fear, he'd learned, because everyone seemed to know everyone else in Iowa, which wasn't a state so much as a vast system of often unreadable, even malevolent, causality, and you could end up on the receiving end of the legal world's version of bad karma so quick, it wasn't even funny. He shivered. He forced himself to breathe deeply, because sometimes it was just the thing. He didn't know what else to say; he asked the priest his name. He didn't really care, and just before V. forgot it, the priest told him, his right hand extended, which V. clasped, if awkwardly, and firmly shook. "Pleasure to meet you," V. managed. Beneath all of this, V. had been searching for a politic—maybe joshing?—way to broach the topic of the bleeding, which seemed to have grown worse. But there were extenuating considerations. To wit: Though the bleeding struck him as an issue important enough to raise, wasn't it even now a little late to be doing so? He was certain that blood loss of this magnitude constituted something by which a minimally sensate and responsible person should *immediately* be taken aback. As in, *Oh, hey! Etc.* Insurance lawyers all the more so. But then, what kind of person—priest, layperson, whatever—*himself* bleeding, went around ignoring other people's blithe insouciance in the face of such a grievous and obvious physical injury?

Was V. exposed in any way?

He didn't know where the words came from, but they came: "Are you—comfortable?"

The priest was monitoring their progress through fields of monotonous soy. A genetically uniform mono crop. He nodded without turning. "Comfortable enough."

V. stopped himself before voicing anything that might be mistaken for tacit stipulation of the bleeding itself. The man's an adult, he thought. He's an adult *priest*, with all the resources of the Roman Catholic Church and the Communion of Saints at his disposal. Calm down. If he needs help from the likes of me, a guy who hasn't seen the inside of a church for decades, he'll ask for it.

The priest turned, suddenly. "What's on your mind?"

V. managed to conceal his shock at so direct an assault, which registered as a disembodied thud against the general low-level dissociation he'd been experiencing for some time now. "Well, the usual, I guess," he said, surprising himself again, with his own moxie this time, with the very tone of his voice. He didn't want to go writing checks with his alleged self-confidence that his timid ass couldn't cash. The blood had so saturated the left side of the priest's jacket, that it seemed to shine in the green light from the dash. The man asked the question—again.

V. felt the familiar surge of mild confusion that sometimes preceded his initial words in court, words he'd practice for days beforehand. Then it was gone: "When they say that—and I'm aware this is stodgy, what? dogma?—that the Virgin Mary was bodily assumed into heaven—"

The priest winced as he sat up straight. "The who?"

"I mean, not that I have any business asking, I haven't been to mass in—"

"Blah. Blah. Blah."

V. wasn't sure he'd heard correctly. He decided he hadn't. "When they say that the Virgin Mary was *assumed bodily into heaven,* what does that *mean* exactly? Because when I hear something like that—"

The priest coughed violently.

"—I sort of zone out," V. said, his voice rising a bit, despite itself, "because, really, how can such an utterance make *any* sense whatsoever? I mean, if language itself can be said to denote anything at all, that is. If we occupy, you and me, the same universe." It was true; he'd wondered about the topic, though not in a long time. Maybe before day's end he'd finally put the issue to rest. Even so, why was he talking like this?

The priest touched the wet spot on his jacket and, working the moisture between forefinger and thumb, held it up to his face and sniffed.

"Isn't heaven—" V. began, faltered deliberately, rhetorically, then pretended to try again: "Didn't Jesus say heaven is at hand?"

The priest smiled thinly, his face on angle. "'The kingdom of heaven is at hand.' Indeed."

"Right, so if it's at hand—" V. held out his right palm. But this time, encountering the priest's alarmingly emotionless expression, he almost faltered for real. All at once the man looked deathly bored.

"Oh, Jesus," he said.

"—and it's not a place—"

"Check yourself." The priest raised an index finger. "Who *the hell* told you heaven's 'not a place'?"

V. could smell the blood now, a kind of secret smell like something at the back of a junk drawer you never opened. He willed himself not to worry about his leather seats. They weren't *his* leather seats. The Lexus was a lease.

"You don't go to your cardiologist to talk root canal," the priest said. He seemed to be addressing the burled wood of the glove compartment.

V. watched him for as long as safe driving allowed.

"Do you go to your cardiologist to talk root canal?"

V. shook his head no. "Are you a cardiologist?"

The priest waved the question aside with a petulant swipe of his hand. "Then what are we talking about here?" He patted the left breast of his black wool jacket, remembering something. His voice gentled. Bending closer, he spoke as though delivering an aside: "Oh, remind me, will you, when we're done with this: I got another favor to ask."

"You bet."

"Anyway, us discussing the finer points of doctrine, back and forth, as though you and I were both adequately informed?

What I've learned over the years. Know what that would be like?" The priest issued a brittle laugh. "Me holding forth on tax law. And you could put everything I know about tax law in this." He held up a tin of Altoids. Original flavor. He snapped open the lid and offered one to V.

"I'm not a tax lawyer." V. cornered a chalky mint. "But I think I see your point."

"So ask yourself, what difference would it make," the priest said, fingering around inside the tin himself now, the wax paper all a-crackle, "my trying to explain to you how and why, after centuries of theological discourse, the Church holds that the BVM is bodily in heaven?"

"BVM?"

He looked over, annoyed. "Blessed Virgin Mother."

"Hey, it might," said V. "Make a difference."

"No, sir." The priest popped an Altoid into his mouth and licked his fingers. "Anyway, I'm not going there, not today. She's in heaven. Her body is. Let's leave it at that. Have a little faith, if not in the doctrine, then in the vestigial power of language to mean what it actually says."

V. made a wincing, foul-smell face. "How, though? How can it—"

"You must have a problem with your hearing," said the priest. "What did I just say?"

V. didn't appreciate the man's tone, at all.

"Look, it's technical, is all I'm saying. Like anesthesiology. It's just as dangerous. And if you haven't put in the time, which forgive me for saying strikes me as obvious in this case, what's the point? It'll go right over your head." He made a zooming sound, his hand weakly motioning at V.'s scalp. "So permit me to give you the standard *take-it-on-faith-leave-the-rest-to-us-and-go-*

on-about-your-business line and we can drop it. Let's enjoy the ride." The priest snapped the Altoids tin shut. There was blood on the white metal, which he spirited away.

"Do *you* believe the BVM's body is in—" here V. made quotation marks in the air with the fingers of both hands, letting go of the wheel for a moment—"heaven?" He regretted the gesture immediately.

The priest looked at his shoes. He shook his head. "What d'you want me to say? Will it make a difference?" He drew a deep breath. "Do you really think it's a question of belief? Yes, OK. *I* believe it. So? How helpful is that?"

V. sighed loudly and rolled his eyes.

"Hey, buddy, spare me the attitude!" the priest said. "You're a man now. It's time to put away childish things. All the 'this-not-that' foolishness. You don't give a rat's ass about the BVM. Move on to other concerns and stop wasting our time." He patted the breast of his jacket again, pushed the bill of his cap back, and looked out at the darkening geometry.

V. was going to say something, his mouth began to move, he even heard the saliva therein snap, but now, amazingly, the priest's hand lay lightly on the right shoulder of V.'s white business shirt. "So," the man said, his tone kindly, "that favor."

V.'s sinuses were alive with the Altoids. He checked the time on the dashboard clock. It was an involuntary motion. The priest followed his eyes to the clock, then back.

"Hey! I don't want to put you out," the priest said, settling into his seat. "You were kind to stop for a stranger."

V. smiled. "Did everyone else just drive by?"

"No," said the priest, "you were the first car I saw."

"Just how far are you going, anyway?" V. asked. "Where can I drop you?" But it came out all wrong, like a challenge.

The priest flashed his eyebrows. "You can pull over right here, goddamn it."

V. was horrified. "No, I didn't mean—"

"Stop right here," he said, firmly. "Pull over."

"I'm going all the way to Des Moines. Really, it's fine."

The priest fumbled with something in the breast pocket of his black jacket. Annoyed, he finally managed to pull it free, dark and heavy, then slapped it onto the slant of the dashboard without taking away his hand, the back of which was smeared with fresh blood. It was a gun.

"Pull over," he said again, his voice half an octave lower this time. "Do it. Now."

V. applied the brakes, the tires barked on the asphalt; and as he angled onto the shoulder, the rumble strip blurted something unintelligible, and the gun cracked forward into the windshield, then dropped into the darkness at the priest's feet. He fished it up, his eyes bright.

"Look—" The priest held the gun by the barrel, the way you'd pass a sharp knife to a child, by the blade. "Take this. Now."

In the quiet, V.'s breath whistled in his nostrils. He flashed to Lazarus, the one who died, the one called forth stinking from the grave, not the rich thirsty guy in hell. "You want me to take that."

"Yes." The priest's attempt at a smile—a squint-eyed grimace full of anguish and loathing—was the worst thing V. had seen so far. "I want you to take it."

V. took the gun, and it was warm. Fascinated, he examined it in his hand. He turned it over. As in a dream. It had a squarish barrel, the word *AUSTRIA* engraved on the side. "And do what with it?"

With some difficulty, the priest drew his left knee up onto

the bucket seat so he could face V. "OK. This is an odd request, I know, but the hour is upon us, and I need another favor. So called." He removed his baseball cap, which had left an architectural dent in his damp dark hair. "I'll just lay it out there. Man to man. You're a lawyer. I'm sure you appreciate plain speech."

Was it a joke?

"Out in that field—" The priest jerked his thumb over his shoulder into the fogged window. Thump. He twisted, his eyes pinched in pain, and widened the dot awkwardly with his palm so they might both see out into the world beyond. But it was too dark now. "It's like this: we walk out a hundred yards from the road. Take an evening stroll. Then, you shoot me in the back of the head." The priest coughed a bloody aerosol into his palm.

"Why?" V. asked.

"Well," said the priest, in the tone reserved for intercourse with idiots, "because I no longer wish to live."

V. couldn't look away. He wanted to. In the dashboard light the priest's eye sockets were green-rimmed and empty. "Why not?"

"You expect me to take you through it? I don't know you from Adam."

V. struggled to avoid a rush to judgment. This guy was a priest and, as such, inscrutable. He must have his reasons. They were a strange tribe, after all. He hefted the pistol in his hand. "Just put it—what?—to the base of your head and—"

"Shoot." The priest leaned stiffly away from V., his chin buried in his chest, and indicated a spot three inches above the collar of his shirt, just above the line of his neatly cut hair. His fingers were slender, almost elegant, his nails manicured to a slight point. "Right there. See? Yeah. Let's get out and away from the road, though. I don't want anyone to see and I'd hate to mess up your interior."

V. looked at the leather seats. *Buttery* was the word the sales-
man had used. They were smeared with blood now, some of it
already brown and dry. "Hey, when I said I was having a hard
time with the doctrine of the Assumption—"

The priest faced him again, his jaw muscles in knots beneath
his circle beard. "You think I'm kidding about this?"

"What am I supposed to think?"

The priest reached for the gun. "Give me that." But V. shifted
his position, the weapon shifting with him, out of the man's
reach. He'd never held one before. The handle had been
machined for exquisite comfort in the palm. Was it loaded? And
how might he know, short of pulling the trigger? In last year's
Christmas-gift name draw at the firm, one of the older part-
ners, cheerful Morrissey, had bought him a black NRA cap and
fake membership card as a gag gift. It had gotten a big laugh.
The gag had worked. Whenever Morrissey came by his office,
V. would whip out the cap and go all Charlton Heston on his
ass, and whatever topic they discussed seemed somehow lighter.
V. wasn't a gun guy. Briefly, just after the invasion of Iraq, in the
patriotic delirium, he'd experienced a passing infatuation with
Second Amendment literalism, imagining himself in a dead-end
exchange of gunfire through broken windows with Bush's para-
military on their roundup of subscribers to *Mother Jones*. But the
roundup had never materialized. He did like the way the gun
felt in his palm.

The priest snatched it away. He ejected the magazine from
the grip, held it up for V. to see that it was, in fact, loaded with
copper-shiny hollow points, then snapped the magazine into
place and pulled back on the cocking mechanism. A series
of quick, deft movements. He turned the gun's dark barrel on
V. "Get out of the car."

A substantive moment of what might be described as tentative silence ensued.

"Father, you're scaring me."

"That's what I'm trying to do," the priest said. "I'm motivated. I want to motivate *you*."

V. yanked on the chrome door latch. The door disengaged. He stepped out. All around, the countryside was vast and black. Above the curved roof of the Lexus, he watched the priest emerge. His face glowed unhealthy and white.

"Come over to this side." He motioned with the gun. Then, softer, as though to himself: "I'm sorry about this."

V. started around the front of the car, then noticed the spill of cabin light on the road and backtracked to shut the door. When he came around again his arms were raised.

"Put them down, for God's sake."

V. lowered his arms.

"Believe me. I wouldn't be taking such extreme measures if—" He pointed the gun across a ditch illuminated by the car's bluish headlights. Cornflowers twitched brightly in the wind. "You first. Out there."

At the edge of the incline, V. hesitated. He recognized what lay before him as an *open-channel ditch,* the term surfacing from years of legal briefs detailing highway spin-outs, people falling asleep at the wheel, carefully worded narratives of absolute mayhem. Often, drivers ended up in one just like this. Drunk, shattered, crippled. Dead. He couldn't see the bottom of the ditch, though he saw well into the rows of soybeans, to the limit of the headlights. Maybe it was alfalfa. He had some questions. He was considering how best to phrase them when he turned to see the priest, much closer now, his eyes crazy-wide and rolling, the gun pointed at V.'s chest. Road grit outlined the wound in the priest's black suit jacket; it sparkled when he breathed.

They said it at exactly the same time: "Please." Neither of them smiled.

"I have a kid and a wife," V. said. He meant it. It felt like he meant it. But there was no wife and no child. There had been, for longer than he could remember, but only in his imagination. In the seam between sleep and waking. Which is to say, he was alone.

"I don't," said the priest.

V. glanced up from the gun. The man wasn't smiling.

"This is awkward," said the priest, "no bout adoubt it." He stumbled after V. into the ditch, then scrambled up out of it, struggling for breath. "But it's really simple, how it's going to work. Then you're on your way. With a story to tell. Not before you shoot me in the back of the head." He swallowed, with difficulty. "I'll waste you if you don't."

They started to walk. Loudly, the priest ran his tongue around the inside of his mouth. A death thirst. V. knew it from the movies. The westerns. The noirs. The legion of gut-shot characters, good or bad, it didn't matter—in their last moments they always pleaded for water. You knew who was a good guy by noting who answered the request. "I can imagine what you're thinking," said the priest. When he showed his teeth again it was just as horrible as the first time. More so. "In five minutes, one of us'll walk out of this field, get in the car and drive away. I'd look silly as hell sitting behind the wheel of a Lexus. Not that I—"

"You mind filling me in on a couple of things?" V. asked. But the priest was too busy high-stepping through the alfalfa to answer. "Maybe I'm missing something, because what if I just turn the gun back on you after you give it to me and then I'll have all the power and I'll just refuse to shoot you?"

The priest stopped to glower at V. from beneath an oily brow. He was trying to keep his balance, his arms spread as though the answer were obvious even to an idiot. "I'll just lunge at you in a rush of blind rage and take it back." Everything about the man said he was serious. "You'll have to shoot me if you want to live."

"Got it." V. nodded. He felt short of breath himself. "OK, then. May I ask you another question?"

"No. No more questions."

"Are you really a priest?"

The man staggered forward, then righted himself. He was trying to stand tall. Close up, he seemed older now, but then V. had known him mostly in profile.

"Society of Jesus?" V. asked.

"Get going."

"What's the theological angle on this, Father?"

"What did I tell you about that stuff?"

"Isn't it a sin—"

The priest stopped walking. He canted left, then right, as though demonstrating in slow motion a dance step far beyond his skill set. He pointed the pistol into the sky and tried to pull the trigger. He could not—not with one hand. "No talking now. Only moving now." He nearly fell backward, but then, righting himself, with both hands on the gun, he managed to squeeze off a shot, the sound of which the sky swallowed with one gulp. "See?"

V. trudged farther into the field. The crop whispered to his ankles. From behind him now came a gurgling in the man's chest. Once again V. fought the impulse to run; for a moment he saw himself sprinting away over black-green fields. Wouldn't the lights along the horizon part like wings to welcome him?

He managed to keep walking, fully under control, the priest moaning and gasping at his heels, until, just beyond the reach of the halogen headlights, he heard the man stumble in the biomass, and V. turned to see him kneeling in the crops, his fingers splayed white on his thighs. A silhouette against the headlights, his shoulders heaving.

V. shuffled closer. With his feet, he fished around in the dark furrows for the pistol, found it, picked it up.

"Give it here," the priest whispered. He'd shed the Brooklyn accent, but he might have been delirious. "And all this could be yours," he said. The phrase seemed to require an accompanying gesture the priest was unwilling or incapable of making.

When V. held the gun out, he was surprised to see it pointed at the priest's head. He waited into a silence made deeper by the hollow roar of a jet airliner miles overhead.

Finally, the priest took a deep breath. "You don't know how to end this, do you?"

That tone again.

"You think you do," the priest said. He laughed a few raggedy syllables, but then his breathing caught up with him like a gang of thieves, and he began to hack and cough.

"Look, just shut up." Still pointing the gun at the man, V. now seemed to be moving toward the car. "Wait there." He had only taken a dozen steps before the field swallowed up the man's coughing as completely as the sky had swallowed the gun shot.

V. heard the growl of the engine as he skidded down into, then up out of, the open-channel ditch, his soles glad for the firm surface of the concrete. He had a plan, the first real one of the evening. Not a whim. A plan. He would angle the Lexus forward into the ditch, first the front right wheel, then the back, down and up the other side and into the field. Easy. And in a moment he was doing just that, the tires crunching soybeans. Not so hard at all, not for someone who knew what he wanted. Next he saw himself pulling the priest, whom he'd find lying face-down and blood-slick in the furrows, by the shoulders up and into the back seat. Screw the leather, V. thought, it had always had a nubuck feel anyway.

Cruising east on the open road again, having doubled back for the turn north toward Iowa City, V. kept one hand on the wheel, one thrown over the seat back as he monitored the priest's painful struggle to breathe, the bitter herbal smell of crushed-foliage blown clear when he'd powered down the windows. Iowa City. Yes. That's where this would all come to its conclusion. In Iowa City.

But it comes as no surprise that things do not shake out that way. No surprise at all. He's been overly optimistic.

In this version, the only one that really counts, we find V. back at the open channel ditch, cursing and rocking against the steering wheel. And the left rear tire did spin with neither traction nor purchase, as the chassis did list forward over the incline. V. punches the transmission into forward, then reverse, forward, reverse, until he catches a whiff of the burnt-electronics smell that has, for him, always seemed to bear with it a mnemonic haze of malfunction and death.

His chest heaving, V. steps from the car. He knows now: there'll be no Iowa City. The cool black night feels like a blessing. Gone is the urgency. And all at once—another blessing?—he's afforded leisure enough and occasion to gaze down upon himself as though from above, a sad little man, to be sure; he's leaning on the quarter panel of a leased Lexus, his damp ankles crossed, and blood on the hem of his pinstriped suit pants. The heat of the idling engine and nothing more having coaxed him out of the dark fields and into the now.

He motions to pat down his pockets for the gun and finds he's been holding it so tightly in his right hand that his fingers ache. It seems heavier—more substantial than he does himself. Not a gun guy? Really? As the warmth from the hood continues its mindless convection, V. waits; for what, he isn't sure. "Be patient," he whispers. "Don't assume anything yet." There's no one asking. He almost wishes there were. He would like to say, aloud—to plead his case?—that he never consciously left the Church, and have someone there to call him out for such a meaningless phrase. Someone to dirty it up with what's real. He cocks his ear against the wind and listens. But there's nothing to hear. Just the black fields all around and the distant lights like glass beads. In this version of the story, it begins to rain. "It is written," he whispers. As the first droplets slap the blacktop and plunk the hood of the car, he thinks he's never in all his life been as aware of his blood, viscous as used motor oil and forcing itself into every capillary. He's only halfway home. There's still time to figure out why he isn't leaking from every pore.

COMMON AREA

He felt as though he were choosing one dream from among many.
There were birds in all of them.

—Robert Stone, *A Flag for Sunrise*

The air traffic controller had always admired Saint Francis of
Assisi's uncomplicated rapport with small birds and animals; on
the walk back from the bar he'd decided to visit the parrots.
These self-possessed birds held their tongues by night and woke
at dawn to startle guests at the bed and breakfast with garbled
approximations of unremarkable daily sounds. Now, in the parlor upstairs, he lifted the cover from one of the hulking cages.
It was an afghan with radial powder-blue piping that he suspected the owner herself had knitted. He liked the owner. She
wore clothes intended for a much younger woman. He admired
that. She served breakfasts of tarts and a variety of overly sweet
things, then followed these up with dessert. She looked fit in
jeans.

The parrot beneath raised its head, groggily. This would be
Rita. The owner had told him the night before that her son
was the only other person alive who could touch this bird. For
years, they'd had a special relationship, her son and Rita. The
air traffic controller had flashed to images of Saint Francis of

Assisi, thin-faced, one bony hand extended to the sparrows, stigma clearly visible. Cage cover in hand, he became aware of his own swaying, churned by the waves of what was possible.

Lodging at the bed and breakfast was his wife's idea. He left that kind of thinking to her. It beat Hampton Inn, but he resented the forced conversation with other guests in the morning, and he avoided the common area. The walls were thin. The first night, lying in the narrow bed next to his wife, he'd worried about the owner's son. He'd heard the floorboards outside the room snap, then fall silent, and imagined he could feel the feathery edge of the man's zone of influence through the wall. This made him nervous about performing the connubial intimacies incumbent upon all married men. The owner's son drank. That was clear. He'd emerge from half-darkened rooms wearing a soiled t-shirt. Perhaps this was a man of inconsistent moral convictions.

The air traffic controller lifted the latch to open the cage and slid the sleeve of his jacket up past his elbow. According to the owner, parrots like these routinely lived beyond a hundred years. Rita was the younger bird, with a long life ahead of her. The air traffic controller was already fifty-one. He ate thirty-minute steel-cut oatmeal in the morning and exercised aerobically; he had that kind of patience. Into the cage went his fist, slowly. He was trespassing. Well within his zone of concern now, Rita fidgeted. They demonstrated wisdom, these birds. People wrote them into their wills. During the day, Rita imitated a land-line telephone and the end-of-recess bell from the grammar school next door. She issued what sounded like spoken English words. The air traffic controller knew better: what made a word a word wasn't only the sound. The night before, the owner had warned him not to insert his finger into the cage. Rita's beak appeared to be made of calcium, formed through a process of accretion like the curve of a nautilus shell. Last night the air traffic controller had stood in this same spot, bourbon fuzzy, and all at once he'd realized the owner didn't trust him. Her words, her glances, her whole manner seemed to call into existence a world of recrimination to swallow him whole. She was a tiny woman with a handsome face and clear eyes. Sassy eyes. With them she'd seen something in the air traffic controller, some flaw in his soul that might lead to cruelty. But the air traffic controller wasn't cruel. He was competent. He kept thousands of people airborne and alive.

Rita understood. They had their own connection.

The air traffic controller commuted forty-five minutes each way to work, rode the elevator to the eleventh floor of a building with small windows in suburban Tampa, not far from a decommissioned section of the air force base. Between shifts, he read widely. Science. Meteorology. Military history. He absorbed language courses on various digital media. Noons, he lunched at Subway with men his age who piloted remote-operated drones into enemy airspace on the other side of the planet. He'd played squash with one of them, only to decide against allowing the friendship to blossom after imagining the man's interior life. The air traffic controller's own zone of operation, the airspace he officially presided over, started small at ground level. There, it stretched just fifty miles across, but ascended in expanding radii to form an inverted wedding cake. He used this analogy at breakfast across from other husbands whom he secretly pitied for their positions as postal clerks or sales associates or small-business owners, and his wife rolled her eyes.

"Rita," he said, "what's the word on the street?" In slow motion, the bird shifted her prehistoric grip along a wooden dowel, edging away from him. She cocked her head. She was dripping with character. When the air traffic controller started to bob in place, Rita bobbed in place as well. "Get down," he whispered. "Show me what you got." Farther into the cage, he piloted his fist. She stopped bobbing and issued a low-pitched rumbling noise akin to human gargling. "Whoa." Shoulders hunched, he listened for stirrings in the house. Nothing. Rita leaned forward, then crept back, teasing him. He slipped his cellphone from his jeans. The night before, he'd been videotaping Rita through the bars of her cage when the owner appeared. Even at work, he had a lot of time on his hands, in between brief shifts. He managed a huge portion of Caribbean airspace. Millions benefited, people he could only envision in dreams, each at the center of a circle, the overlapping edges bluish-green. He called up the video of Rita and faced the phone toward her like a mirror she might peer into. Perched at the threshold of the cage, she need only lean forward to stroke the smooth surface of the phone with her calcified carapace of a beak. She seemed bored. The video ended. The air traffic controller wiped the phone on his jeans, put it away, and offered Rita his wrist. "It's your call," he said. She angled an eye at him, at his wrist, then inched onto the bump of it, her talons needling his skin. "I'm not cruel, Rita," he said. "I'm patient." Rita seemed to understand. He focused. He tried to sensitize himself to her zone, which he imagined extending a few inches from the center of her being, where whatever it was that looked out through her eyes resided. From there, if it existed, it would radiate out beyond her downy outline into the realm of worldly contingencies. But he saw nothing like that. Rita lowered her iridescent head as though inviting him to caress the soft blue-green region above her beak. Like a lover. But he was cautious. The owner had done exactly this the night before, even as she'd issued warnings; and when he tried it now, Rita bobbed left, then right, a slow-motion dodge, like something from the age of silent film. Years from now, this bird, this very Rita, would remember the air traffic controller. He'd be dead. All the people he'd kept safe would be dead. Not Rita. He offered up the bony fulcrum of his knuckle, against which she might scratch herself. He wasn't going to rush her. She could come to him. But she must have grown confused, despite her limitless wisdom, because she raised her beak in a swift, thoroughly natural motion, clamped onto the fatty bulge below his knuckle, and opened a beak-shaped gash. She hopped to the room's only wing-backed chair to look back at him. He whistled an in-suck, cupped his hand, and turned toward the hallway light. "Damn, girlfriend." There was a triangular flap, a little trapdoor of flesh and pulp, like the in-curled isosceles he'd punched into cans of Hi-C as a child. There was no pain yet. The blood welled thick and viscous, spilling into his other palm then over to drip and bead on the oriental rug's elaborate patterns. At first, he had the presence of mind not to move. He resisted the airy panic of too-eager pourers of champagne surprised by the volume of bubbly. He took his finger in his mouth and tongued the wound. It tasted the way licking the nodes of a nine-volt battery felt, tangy.

Rita's entire manner suggested a profound lack of concern. Her own dry tongue appeared for a moment. With it she seemed to lick her lips. But parrots didn't have lips. They had beaks. Hers was limned with red. Stiffly, the air traffic controller stepped into the lavatory off the parlor and with his elbow tripped the light switch. He stood over an antique porcelain sink, all spidered with brownish cracks, and watched it spot with red. With the meat of his good hand, he twisted the cold water on and let the clean stream rinse the blood from his finger in curled strings. He pulled a hand towel from a silver loop and fashioned a bandage that wound around and around to end in a fat cotton mitt that he held up for inspection. He felt calm, but this didn't surprise him. Whatever his own circle touched, even for a moment, it left calmer, more itself.

In the parlor Rita clung to the converging bars at the crown of her cage. She scratched her head with her free claw. She lifted a wing to dislodge parasites with her enormous beak. The air traffic controller listened again for stirring in the house. He unraveled the bandage, and the gore surged again like fresh jewelry. He found a clean towel and tightly rewrapped the wounded finger. "I see what you mean, Rita," he said to himself. "I hear you." Back in the parlor, he watched the bird maneuver with the steadying grip of her beak into the cage. What did the taste of human flesh do to a parrot? "Enough said."

He snapped the door shut, lifted the cage from its hook, set it on the rug to drape the knit cover. With his good hand, his boots avoiding the blood spatter on the rug, he carried the cage out onto the hallway's polished hardwood, down the stairs, then into the wider space of what the owner called the common area. The wound in his finger seemed fully awake now. It seemed to be transmitting in a code he'd forgotten along telegraph wires that loped to the farthest outposts of what he was. Near the threshold to the den, he felt a ripple, a fluctuation he associated with the intersection of zones. There he saw, slumped on the couch, the owner's son, whose overcoat had ridden up to his waist, whose chin rested in a pool of his own neck flesh.

"Which one you got there, champ?" A puffy man, he didn't take up a lot of space. He was younger than the air traffic controller by fifteen years. They looked like contemporaries.

The air traffic controller raised the cage and cleared his throat. "Rita, I think."

"You mean Kiwi." The owner's son sat up.

"No. It's Rita."

"I don't know where you come up with Rita. There's Kiwi and Wink." He reached for a square unlabeled bottle on a side table. His wet eyes on the air traffic controller, he drew a slow, significant draft. "She nip you?"

The air traffic controller lifted the mitt of his fist.

"Sweet Jesus." The owner's son stood, approached, slowed, smiled. "Did you stop off on the way home?" There was mockery in his voice.

"We haven't been formally introduced."

"Where you taking my bird?" The man seemed to remember the bottle in his hand. He offered it to the air traffic controller, whose own hands were full. Then he crouched, carefully, to lift the cover. "You got Kiwi here. She's not partial to this cover. Too hot. Not enough air gets in. She don't like it."

"That's your bird." The air traffic controller tried to smile. "The one you—"

"They're *both* my birds. *Our* birds. Me and my mother's."

"You have something with Rita. A certain special something. Between you."

"Let's get some air."

"A rapport." He thought he could see it now, the uneven frontier of the man's zone, shifting, glimmering.

The owner's son stood blinking at him. "Put the cage down."

"I wouldn't hurt Rita."

"It's Kiwi. Put the cage down."

The air traffic controller glanced at his bandaged hand, thinking he might see his wounded finger charged and burning through the fabric of the towel, its own species of light leaking out. "I apologize. I left a little blood on the rug up there."

"Up where?"

"In the parlor. On the rug."

"You've had a few. You stopped off."

Neither of them had noticed the owner. Now it was too late. She stood in the hall in a tartan robe, her hair up, her arms crossed, her thin white shins below.

"Oop," said her son.

She looked from one man to the other and back. "What'd I tell you?" she said finally, to the air traffic controller. There was power in her eyes. "You stuck your finger in the cage."

Not the whole story, but the air traffic controller wasn't going to get into it all, the complicated world. "I did," he said.

"How bad she get you?" she asked. A granny and a looker all in one. A seer into his uncluttered soul. Then: "Where you taking my bird?"

The owner's son fussed with a boxy lump in his t-shirt pocket. "Him and I were going out for a smoke."

But the owner continued to glare at the air traffic controller, even after he'd set the cage down between them. Her eyes were unbearable. People were dying on the other side of the world, he wanted to say, flickering out, failing. Here we were bickering over birds. In Florida. So be it, he wanted to say. Lesson learned. He'd never touch another parrot in his life. Decades hence, in homes not yet built by people not yet born, Rita would grow strong on the memory of his blood. He'd live on, in that way. The owner stepped forward. The air traffic controller edged back, as though to stay just outside her zone of significance. But her zone of significance was as undeniable as it was vast. And by now he knew its edges extended well beyond the X-ray frame of the great house.

SINKHOLE

She was forty-five. She owned a modular home on a quarter acre three blocks east of a small strip mall with a CrossFit gym, a recently defunct Thai restaurant, and a curiosity shop. She owned the curiosity shop. At one time—she could still remember, it wasn't that long ago—there had been a brisk market for curiosities. Popular curiosities had included taxidermied hairless cats; two-headed sheep; two-headed goats; one-headed goats in nineteenth-century night frocks; goats—also single headed— meditating cross-legged in pajamas; various human skulls harnessed up to leathern neck braces; bowls of marsupial penises ("bone in"); glittering split geodes; one fetus (human) curled and suspended in a thick-glass jar of formaldehyde. Much more. Sales were slumping. Demand for the putative ingredients for witches' brew—e.g., "newts"—had entered a period of decline. The wiccans had aged, lost interest.

Other, exogenous factors obtained. As they do.

One local nondenominational pastor heard tell of the fetus, which became a topic of, at times, heated discussion before and after Sunday and Wednesday services and during Bible study, also on Wednesday. The pastor urged participants to seek scriptural justification for direct action re the fetus. He encouraged the spirited recitation of scripture, then counseled patience while the few in regular attendance waited to be convicted. Conviction did occur. An argument emerged along the following lines:

That jarred fetus in the curiosity shop was a human being.

Was?

Is!

Today, she stood in the doorway of the curiosity shop. Sunlight fell through leagues of humid atmosphere to reach her, and the hairless shop cat writhed at her feet, very much alive, its worsening central nervous system disorder manifesting in tremors of uneven amplitude, the overall impression of which, at their worst, suggested a creature from the era of flickering Ray Harryhausen movies. The pastor stood opposite her, a few steps lower. She showed no emotion. She felt no emotion. She had worked in retail for decades as both employee and, of late, as employer. The latter wasn't capitalism, per se, except perhaps for the dependence on a fickle "free market." This was self-employment. As her "own boss" she exercised sole discretion with regard to the distribution of what Marx called the value of the surplus labor, *surplus labor* being labor performed above and beyond *necessary labor,* which was the labor necessary to provide for the needs of the laborer in question. She knew that self-employment (or what Marx called "The Ancient Way") was one of only two non-exploitative economic modes. The other was, of course, socialism.

See that fetus in that jar?

The pastor could have been anyone. She had never seen the man. Did it matter? His sleeves had been rolled. He'd probably rolled them himself. His arms were sinewy. As was his mouth. (The word *rictus* came to her, unbidden.) The bottom third of his face seemed whiter than the rest, as though he'd recently shaved a beard. This was speculation. When he was not pointing, he was propping his hands on his hips, elbows spread, and he wore tan slacks and a white uniform shirt (of the aforementioned rolled sleeves) with a thin brown tie. And, most importantly, this: his face bore witness to an ongoing battle—a *spiritual* battle, yes, preach—between an impulse toward heated declarations of righteousness, and the frisson—no other word—to accompany any resultant pride. Yes. How satisfying. Pride. At having the courage to confront the source of the impulse toward righteous declaration. Circular.

Crowding him from behind, fifteen or so fully engaged religious—men and women, one of them holding a dazed and sunburned child on her hip.

That fetus? In the jar?

She didn't have to turn. She knew where the fetus was. She turned anyway. The jar rested on a back-wall shelf in a shaft of diagonal sunlight, which charged the formaldehyde with an exacerbating glow, *exacerbating* in that it worsened an unavoidable impression regarding the skin of the fetus, of smooth unwholesomeness and soggy nubuck leather. The pastor wished it to be known that he was upset. His people were upset. His people. They had *walked* along the strip malls from the church at some distance—many showed signs of perspiration—and had arrived only moments earlier wreathed in a spirit of patience and magnanimity. Whereupon another spirit had descended. The pastor tried to smile.

This isn't the future yet.

She had no idea what that might mean, what function it might serve other than as a cogent illustration of tautological redundancy.

We don't sell human beings anymore. And when they're dead—the human beings we don't sell—we still bury them. Even the Neanderthals buried their dead.

Taken aback by the pastor's tacit acknowledgment of a key tenet of human evolutionary history (weren't these guys against all that?), still, she could see his point. She surveyed the makeshift gathering. Strangers, all, in modest dress, attire suitable for employment at a big-box retail store. She wasn't sure she didn't see her own future at Walmart. A youngish man in the rear raised his chin, his eye sockets thrown into deepest shadow. It occurred to her that (1) the unspoken premise of the pastor's argument—along with the indignation that fueled it—was of a piece with the very sentiment that drew patrons, many of whom bought *nothing,* to the curiosity shop. And that (2) the long waning of this sentiment—or of the ethos that made it possible—lay behind the curiosity industry's general decline. Conjecture, perhaps.

But was there anything else she could do for him?

He stepped back. *This isn't the future yet.*

Every eye held her as though suspended above. Every right hand held a green, pocket-sized New Testament.

"Not yet," she said.

* * *

An hour later she walked through her modular home without touching a thing—unlike the curiosity shop, there was hardly anything to touch—and without putting down her bag on the kitchen table moved out into the small backyard, across which ran an entirely imaginary line separating her property from her neighbors'. These neighbors, an older couple of nonspecific age or ethnicity, owned a food truck they left at night in the corner of a Home Depot parking lot two miles along the same arterial avenue on which could be found the curiosity shop. Out toward Orange Blossom Trail. OBT. They owned this land, here, but did they really? Could you ever own it—or any other land? How about the moon? A phrase—*property is theft*—tried to surface from the lower regions. One of her ratty aluminum lawn chairs had been dragged across the imaginary line. Maybe the wind. She dragged it back, turned it toward her own modular home, sat down to imagine the provenance of legal ownership of this her parcel of "Florida." And what exactly was "Florida"? Did it exist? She doubted it, though the conceptual and logical preconditions for "existence" were a dense thicket to be sure. As a child she had asked her priest if God was real, at which the old man had smiled, sat back, and replied, *Is He real? Yes. Does He exist? No.*

It was, perhaps, the same with Florida. But what about the fetus? No. Did that make any sense? No. There was no connection.

* * *

The pastor no longer listened to radio news but craved instead a decorous silence. Morning by morning, before driving to the church, with his morning milk he had, from the small balcony of his apartment, monitored the expansion of the sinkhole. The sun now low on the western horizon, the shadowed contours of the depression grew more pronounced in evening relief. Every day he would return from church to find that the landscaping crew across the way had positioned the orange caution cones further apart. Every day they were working. They were always working. Saturday, even Sunday. One night the caution tape had appeared. Like a crime scene. The last sunlight glinted on the water percolating up from the sinkhole's center and disappearing beneath its edges. He believed he lived in "old Florida," if there ever had been such a place, or he occasionally nursed a half-formed desire along those lines. The landscaping crew worked for the new apartment building across the gully, in the parking lot of which expensive cars with license plates from Ohio and New Jersey glistened. Something was leaking, bleeding out. He would awake at 4:00 a.m. and lie without rising and without prayer, and watch the light come up, and listen as the sparrows found their voices. He would ache for a cigarette, still, a vestige of a former life whose passing he publicly celebrated as the context for a story he often sermonized. He wasn't a normal pastor. Not on the inside. Something, you could call it God, had found him despite himself. How surprising that things could change: that this was the unfolding history of his finding himself alone, with God, all things moving forward, riverlike. And along with this God's blessing—His apparent many-staged plan for the pastor—came, it seemed, new awareness of the contradictory nature of time: how fleeting, how light, and yet how brutal, in the end. No, the truth would never preach.

He walked back through the apartment, into the hallway, through the evening sounds of his neighbors, the evening smells, of dinner, of cigarette smoke and of marijuana, down the concrete stairwell, suddenly cooler, and back out into the humid air. The sinkhole lay beyond a chain-link fence that ran along the edge of his apartment building's hem of concrete, where people carried the day's bagged trash to brightly colored plastic containers. He leaned against the fence, felt its sag and creak. Matthew 7:24. Or was that too obvious? Though maybe there was something in it, a twist, a good twist. Even if you built your house on rock, or on as solid a patch of ground available, what then?

Into a diamond-shaped opening in the fence, he pressed the toe of one of the black shoes he had bought for a song at Savers, and lifted himself onto the top rail, swung his other leg over, and found himself standing in the grass. Soft. Cushiony. He approached the sinkhole. There was a backhoe. He slowed to run his hand over its rear bucket, the warm steel still radiating the day's accumulated sunlight.

"You looked worried," someone said. He turned. A woman leaned against the fence. She was holding a plastic garbage bag. He'd seen her before. She lived in the building, alone. He had tried on more than one occasion to imagine the story of another life that might lead here, to this building. Her life. He could not.

"Not sure that's the right word," he said. "Worried."

"You're a pastor."

"Am I?"

"So how can you be worried? Isn't worry the opposite of faith?"

He frowned, examined his scuffed black bargain shoes in the tall grass, looked up at the woman. She was smiling. She wore a waitperson's uniform—black pants, black button-down with the red logo of one of the area's many chain restaurants above the left breast pocket. Chipotle's maybe.

He'd long suspected that God was simply the name history had assigned to the utter strangeness of this world.

"I'm not worried."

"You sound worried."

"About what?" he asked, half turning. "The sinkhole?"

She drew on her cigarette. "About something."

Confronted by people, he almost always faced, if at times unconsciously, an inner struggle. Alone, during the course of a day, he could forget how dead he was. He preferred it that way. In conversation—any encounter beyond the transactional, at the 7-Eleven, the gas pump—the deadness rushed back. At church it was unavoidable. There was a word, but he'd forgotten it, maybe one with Latin roots. It was a gift, this condition, supposedly, a first step on the path through the desiccated wood. Even raging rivers went dry.

She seemed to sense a need in him, an urge, dropped the garbage bag, found the pack of cigarettes in her apron, held it in his direction.

"What does it pay?"

"Pay," he said, walking now toward the pack.

"Being a preacher."

"You want a figure?" he asked, cigarette between his lips now.

Her expression did not change. He would not ask her for a light. She did not offer one.

"After taxes?" he said.

Should he invite her to church? That's what real preachers did. The shepherding of souls. Etc.

"Just a question," she said, flatly.

"Not much."

Though she still stood there, before him, she was already gone.

★★★

The owner of the curiosity shop had not been to the beach in years. When the thought occurred to her, that she might go, to the beach, her mood lifted, in the Civic, on the drive to Publix for frozen French fries and overpriced cigarettes. Did Publix sell cigarettes? At the traffic light at OBT she slowed. The young beggars were working the intersections. They were everywhere. No matter which lane you occupied, if you were in the first five or so automobiles, the beggars with their cardboard signs would find you. Mostly men. The lights here cycled slowly.

She recognized one of them. Up ahead, he bent to each driver's window with the pained and practiced expression of heroic exhaustion. Pitiable but not beyond hope. Some of them carried ironic or bleakly humorous signs—*to ugly to turn trix, I wont lie its for beer*—but this man held a blank sign, a brown cardboard rectangle. Whenever she saw him, she always found $2. She did again, emptied the little tray of quarters, her window down when he arrived.

He smiled through perfect teeth. He was not an unattractive man, though dressed in the uniform of his trade: artfully soiled white t-shirt, droopy jeans with ragged bellbottoms.

"On your way to the beach?" he asked, then stepped away as her car began to roll forward.

"No," she said.

"You should be."

"If I had time."

"Maybe you should make time."

She wanted him to know that she understood what was going on. Not experientially—she had no history of the kind of poverty that drove you to beg for dollars at the busier intersections—but theoretically, which, after all, was not nothing. Economics was the loam. Everything grew from it. Everything. The elite classes had entered the smash-and-grab phase of late-stage capitalism, having turned, just as Marx had predicted, to the last frontier, where the real money was, in this case the U.S. Treasury, which they would raid and empty, and then everyone would finally be on his own, not just the ragged dudes with leathery skin and grime-shiny jeans, but the people who thought a 401k was all the buffer they needed, their naïve faith in quaint illusions like Social Security finally laid bare.

She smiled and accelerated into the intersection.

When he arrived at church he noticed a single car in the parking lot. The Ford Fiesta belonged to his most devout congregant. A lapsed Catholic who worked at Disney, though in what capacity, even after all this time, he did not know. She may have been a "performer" who wore one of those character costumes, a minor extra in the ambulant carnival of Mickey or Dopey or Donald Duck. Maybe an elf, though she'd probably avoid such work out of a now-quaint objection to the secularization of Christmas in the form of elves and Santa and Mrs. Claus and the ritual orgy of consumerism. A tenuous connection, to be sure. It almost did not matter. She had her obsessions. The innate sinfulness of certain genres of music (anything with jazz saxophone), the deep feeling of conviction she felt about her apathy—or helplessness—in the face of the spread of secular humanism. Most of the time he had nothing for her, maybe a verse or two. Still, he had been appreciative of her discovery of the church's newest potential cause—over at the curiosity shop—which she referred to, with relish, as an abomination. The fetus in a jar. She had come into his office with a full-bodied expression of anxiety, not unusual for the woman. He recognized this as another vestige of her Roman Catholic upbringing, with its mixture of unabashed idolatry (Mary, saints, the pope, et al.) and wall-to-wall shaming, always the shaming, especially with regard to matters sexual. She had wanted to confess to him, as usual, and was once more crestfallen that he'd taken time to catalogue the key doctrinal differences between Catholicism and those of the non-denominationalism his church—now her church—embraced. Yes, the two churches did share an abhorrence for the genocide currently underway in the western world—though perhaps not to the same degree. On her way out, unsatisfied as always, she had turned back to him. She was a short woman in her late fifties. Here it comes, he'd thought. But wait, something new. She'd been to the curiosity shop, had gone in there against her better judgment, but her Ohio cousin lived across town now and it was her birthday and the woman had odd tastes. They carried witchcraft supplies. Was it a sin? Even to enter such an establishment?

"Not likely," he said. But that was a matter for her own relationship with Jesus.

"Something convicted me." She had the face of a woman twenty years older. Lined with worry. If this woman had found not even marginal solace in the church, his church—

"At the curiosity shop?"

"Yes," she said. "That woman, the owner, there's something about her."

"Put it in God's hands," he said.

"There's a fetus in there. You know that, right?"

"At the curiosity shop?"

"In a jar, yes. I don't know why. I don't know why someone would buy such a thing."

"Do you know for sure if it's real?"

She nodded. "It looks real. But I was so upset, when I saw it, that first time—the only time—I started to shake, with anger. I just had to leave."

"And now you feel convicted."

"Yes," she said. "We are here to protect the unborn. That's our primary purpose. Right?"

"Yeah," he said.

"It's like what they do at the hospitals with our tax dollars. How they throw aborted babies in trash bags labeled *biohazard*? And here this woman has a beautiful baby in a jar with yellow fluid on a shelf, selling it like it's a stuffed animal or conversation starter."

He watched her with dispassionate eyes, reminded suddenly of his own emptiness, unconnected to her or anything, as though looking into this world from another. Or already dead. Or from a world inside this world, from behind the same kind of thick glass. He felt nothing. He knew he should. He did not. And hadn't that been one of his most stinging criticisms of the mainstream church? Dead?

"What do you think we should do?" she asked.

He knew she knew what he would say. He watched her forehead, facially configuring for her an expression that might indicate a paternalistic trust in the progress of her ongoing spiritual growth.

"Pray on it?" she'd asked.

He'd said he would bring it to the attention of the congregation. She had given him a half smile, and he felt a vague shift in his mood, a ripple in the viscous medium between them.

So today, seeing the Fiesta in the lot, he had the urge to drive on. He could. He had no boss, no report-to but the Lord, who, it was widely known, had long ago adopted something of a hands-off managerial approach. He decided to try something: to pray for openness ahead of the encounter. Or it *occurred* to him. He did not.

She was sitting in a chair in the corner of his office when he came in, but he only felt her presence because he saw, immediately, the fetus. Still in its jar. He paused in the middle of the threadbare carpet. He had never seen it close up before. The room was dark. He turned to her.

"I drew the curtains," she said. "Should we take it out?"

"Out?"

"Yes. Of the jar," she said, "to bury it."

He turned back to the fetus with an unfamiliar calm, beneath it a whiff of self-conscious pride at being so calm. Because wasn't he a pastor for this moment? For today's world? Ready for anything? He approached the fetus, bending for closer inspection. Curled, suspended, illuminated by the only light in the room, the green-shaded lamp on the desk.

She said, "That's a human being, pastor."

He lowered himself into the chair behind the desk. Moisture—condensation, he hoped—had stained his blue desktop blotter, on which she'd placed the jar.

"It's heavy," she said, standing.

"Yes."

"Try lifting it."

"I believe you." He didn't know what to make of his voice.

She turned the jar, inched the lamp closer. "See? He's smiling."

"You *bought* this?"

"No!" she said, taken aback. "We don't buy and sell human beings, pastor. This isn't the future, not yet."

He tried to smile. "So how did it come to be here on my desk?"

"I parked down the street, in the Arby's, so no one would see my car. I walked. I went in through the back."

He asked when.

"This afternoon. I went by to look at it, but the shop was closed, so I parked at Arby's and walked back. I felt convicted. It was easy to get in."

The fetus did appear to be smiling, its greenish flesh made greener by the green lamp. He thought to throw open the curtains. He'd never seen a fetus. This one looked unreal—perhaps it was. A rubberized gag in poor taste. Maybe that was the point.

"Pastor?"

He met her eyes. They were wet, wide, proud, joyful almost.

"It was hard to carry all the way back to the car, but I put it in a big sack I found in the store"—she pointed to a hill of bunched material on the rug—"and tied the ends. Nobody saw. But what if they did?"

"OK," he said, "so technically, that's breaking and entering. It's theft. These are crimes."

Her mood darkened. "It was crime to take this miraculous child in the first place—"

"Do we know the circumstances?"

"—one of God's children and put it in a jar."

He watched her burning in the low light. Her eyes on his.

"Was it a crime when John Brown raided the arsenal at Harper's Ferry?" she asked. "You don't remember your sermon?"

"I never gave a sermon on John Brown."

"You don't have to be involved. I prayed, I felt convicted, like you told us to, and I'll do it."

"Do what?"

"What do you think, pastor?"

"I'll take care of it," he said. He heard the flatness in his voice. Flat. Flatter than usual.

"That's you in that jar. That's me. There's no difference. What are you going to do with it?"

"Right now?" he said, standing, "I'm going to put it in the closet."

"The closet?"

"Don't you work on Thursday nights?"

"You're saying I did wrong, pastor."

"I'm not saying that."

She seemed capable of anything. Standing there.

"I'll take care of it," he said.

After she left, he tried the lid of the jar, which, it seemed, had been sealed with wax or some other crudely effective nineteenth-century adhesive. This was no gag. At the bottom of the jar swirled strings of ancient organic matter. He went out and locked the doors to the church, returned to his office, and sat down. The air conditioning hummed, and he waited, with the fetus, until after sundown to carry it out to his car.

* * *

After Publix, she followed the backroads east, the sun already high, the AC roaring, the road whining beneath her. She had in mind not the boredom of the beach but the open country along a strip of cracked asphalt north of Titusville. There as a child on a daytrip with her father to watch one of the last Apollo liftoffs, she'd been aware of presences coming out from the darkness beneath low palms and scrub to hover over their parked car, and now she wondered if, thirty-seven years later, the feeling would return. A whim. No specific destination otherwise. She was a materialist. What was a "presence"? Nothing real.

Halfway, she stopped for boiled peanuts and gator jerky at a roadside stand set back in the shade. The owner, an old man in a tank top without an ounce of body fat, didn't speak, not even when she smiled in class solidarity, the two of them having avoided, as self-employed people, exploitation at the hands of the dominant economic system. The whole transaction complete in under a minute, she continued east. Half a mile ahead, blurred and insubstantial as a watercolor in the rising air, more than once, this scene: buzzards tearing at the stringy ligaments of roadkill. As she approached, they'd pump their hideous wings, lift off, vectoring low, then swoop up to roost in the bare branches. In the rearview, they'd settle back to their roasting gristle. She passed neglected cemeteries and swampy wastes. Culverts, the flash of white herons, motels pink and defunct, their crushed-shell parking lots strewn with crabgrass. For the moment, the humid world outside more an idea than anything that could actually touch her. Then, finally, she shot out into the wide open and onto a causeway bridge rising like a shimmering ramp to the sky.

But Route 3 was nothing like she'd remembered it. The flatlands on either side lay charred by recent wildfire. Eventually, she pulled to the shoulder, stepped out into the dense convection and near-silence. She walked along the breakdown lane toward a roadside cross. A distant blackened palm stood over the wastes. It had been near here, if not at this exact spot. Other families had camped out to the south, made a day of it, sharing barbecue and potato salad, but her father had sought the silences away from crowds, to more deeply savor the rocket's incongruous interruption of an otherwise normal Florida afternoon. The day had been clear. They sat in beach chairs in the green just off the road surface, waiting, talking every so often. And she remembered thinking, This is a now. A now. It would be a *now* at the moment of liftoff, of course, everyone knew that, but it was a *now* even now. She didn't know what it had meant, one of those absurd insights children used to have but wisely kept to themselves. That's when the presences began to gather. Whirling, swirling, dancing even. Her father held a sweating bottle of Miller High Life. He raised it golden to his lips, his eyes on the southern sky. A now. Like any other now, but different. It was Sunday. Her mother was at church. Her father had removed his watch and fastened it to the arm of the chair. She was seven, but it was the day before her eighth birthday. A day in April. There were still seasons then, in Florida.

The sound of the radio at her father's feet changed. There was a hush, then the countdown. "Get ready," he said. He was a kind man. He worked at a distillery without air conditioning but only drank beer, on Sundays. Inside the system, it was what you did. He never knew he'd had a choice. With the countdown, the presences seemed to slow and settle, as if not to miss what was coming. "Are you watching?" There was a soft uneven rumble, like a deep cough deprived of oxygen.

"See it?" her father said, standing, pointing. "There it is."

★ ★ ★

Almost home, she stopped at the curiosity shop, where, upon opening the door, she sensed immediately that something wasn't right. She left the lights off, walked slowly into the space, listening, her mouth open, her breathing calm and even—so as not to contaminate the silence. The dry food she'd left for the hairless cat was untouched. She clicked her tongue and called for him. "Ray," she whispered. She knew he wasn't there. She searched anyway—under the low stands and tables, beneath the one- and two-headed goats. "Ray." Lately she had been leaving him at the shop. His central nervous system disorder had progressed, and sometimes his tremors would wake her in the night and she'd find him standing over her in the bed, expressionless, his hairless skin, his eyes twitching as he tried to keep her centered in his field of vision. There was no cure. In the back hallway she stopped calling his name and pushed aside the hanging glass beads into the back room. There, beneath a rough wooden pallet, Ray often found refuge from annoying customers. She knelt, pressed her cheek to the cold cement floor. The beads clacked softly. "Ray," she whispered. Ray wasn't there. Rising, she noticed a faint aura of vertical light, saw that the back door stood ajar by an inch. Someone had been in the shop.

Out front, she checked the register. On good days, she still made the deposit at her bank along OBT, but there weren't many good days anymore; deposits had winnowed to a weekly ritual. The cash—small change, she knew the amount—was still there. If she stood in the middle of the room, as still as possible, her mind empty, she thought that she might know what had happened. That it would come to her who had been there. That intuition, sensitivity to things unseen, might be real. Instead, she walked out into the parking lot—"Ray," she called again and again—then, her shadows lengthening, around to the strip of broken asphalt behind the store. Beyond the chain-link fence a green undeveloped lot, riotously overgrown. She imagined Ray lying motionless among the crisps of dried palms and leaves, the molted skins of nonvenomous snakes, the living chameleons.

Late that night she sat in the dark behind her modular home, a white-wine spritzer with strawberries and sweet basil on the table beside her, sweating. She couldn't see the stars, not even the brightest ones, but she could hear the couple in the house across the lawn, across the imaginary property line, their voices and the careful sound of silverware and dinner plates being washed and dried and put away. Work. For hours, the kitchen window glowed yellow with tungsten light. She couldn't hear what they were saying, just the cadences of their conversation. The lulls and quickenings. When the lights finally went out except for the blue glow of a television, the talking continued, slower now, the intervals in the dialogue—and the soft overlapping laughter—lengthening to silence.

★ ★ ★

At about that same time—late, late—the pastor stood on the lawn behind his apartment building. His hand had again found the warm steel of the backhoe's rear bucket. In the dark grass at his feet, the jarred fetus. Next to it, the jar's lid, which he'd removed on his kitchen table after softening the wax seal with a hair dryer, all the while trying not to look at the fetus. In his tight kitchen the smell had been unavoidable. The lid was of the same heavy nineteenth-century glass as the jar, and its handle, a small glass globe, gathered and curled what light there was now. Overhead, ragged clouds glowed unearthly orange as they rushed eastward. In the breeze, the caution tape fluttering like wings, the pastor listened for the gurgle of water in the sinkhole.

MEAT

The blood smeared on Norbert's snout was dark and oily, so whatever he and his crew had been eating was probably dead when they found it. That morning last week he'd come trotting out of the woods as far as the semicircle of trouble lights I'd set up on posts so I could get some painting in before dawn. He threw a glance over his shoulder at what was happening behind him in the blue-blackness, where six or seven mangy-looking dudes chomped mouthfuls of innards and cracked bones. Lately, he and the pack had been looking thin and wobbly. So I was glad they were eating. (Just because I'm denying myself, doesn't mean everyone else has to.) When he looked up at me again, a smile played on his uneven pink and black lips, and I had the impression I was keeping him from something. *Hey, go knock yourself out, dog,* I wanted to tell him, *I have plenty of work to do myself,* but lately we've been talking about some things important to me, and I've come to value his advice. The main important thing concerns my making a move to an academic library, maybe in a college town again, some place like Ann Arbor or Madison, Wisconsin. "What's that really all about?" Norbert asked. "Aren't you happy?"

"You mean here?" I said, looking around. "Sure, I like it here."

But my voice was unconvincing, even to me. The breeze shifted direction; over the sweetness of the latex primer, I caught a sulfurous whiff of rotten meat. "What about you?" I asked. "Are you happy?"

"Right now, we're not talking about me," he said. "Right now, we're talking about you. Are you happy? Answer the question."

I set my brush on the edge of the paint can and my coffee cup on the small platform I'd rigged between the arms of the stabilizer. I was trying to smoke, paint, and drink coffee all at once. Usually, I'd have been eating a bagel, but I'm trying to slim down and maybe find Jesus by fasting, though not necessarily in that order. The house, a "splanch," has fallen into a state of near decay, from the foundations to the gutters. (My wife and son and I have lived here for a decade.) I never put much into it. Time or money. Or thought.

"I don't know." With the lights and the audience and the elevation, it felt like I was on stage. "What's happy?"

Norbert's eyes were silvery drill bits. "Oh, come on. Happy is *happy*. I can't say what that word means for you, old son." In the tungsten glow of the trouble lights, he seemed covered in dandelion blow. Whenever the wind rose, snatches of fur drifted out of sight. It was molting season.

"Seriously, what's it mean for you?" I asked.

Twisting back on himself, he gnawed at his belly, then paused to issue to his crew a succession of yips and bawls not so different from what you'd hear out of a golden lab chained in someone's backyard. The response from his boys sounded more like nervous human laughter. "For me," he said, "*happy* has a lot to do with meat."

Meat. It made sense.

He said, "I can see you're not one for the grill," then nodded at the old hibachi below me on the deck, its black cover in faded shreds. "What do you do, broil it up? Fry it? You don't boil it, do you?"

"I haven't eaten red meat in ten years." The sorrow in my voice surprised me. I took a pointless sip of cold coffee. "I'm a vegetarian, Norbert."

His tail stopped swishing, and he wobbled back dramatically into the shadows as though he'd been smacked. Out there in the darkness behind him, the loud mastication of his peers ceased.

I nodded, a little embarrassed. "Yeah, it's true."

He regained his composure as well as his position at the edge of the circle of light. "That surprises me, Gray."

"Well, I mean, how long have we known each other?" I smiled. "There's a lot to learn." An even stranger silence followed. "So," I said to my paintbrush. "Meat, huh?"

"Meat," he repeated, nodding fondly. He did something with his jaws that started as a grimace but ended as a yawn that showed his full set of pointy yellow teeth. "Yes, indeed."

"You're obsessed with it, I would think. Can't get enough." I dipped the brush in the primer and smoothed over one of holes I'd scraped and sanded the week before. When he didn't say anything, I pressed him: "Am I wrong? Hey, what do I know?"

He'd been thinking it over. "I wouldn't say I'm *obsessed* with it. We might as well be precise. *Obsessed* doesn't fit this context. It's like saying you and I are *obsessed* with breathing."

"Right," I said, "you and I." Yet again we'd returned to a favorite subject of late, concerning our similarities, across species. (That and the crazy suggestion he made from time to time that I adopt him.) "So much in common. Let me count the ways." I paused for effect. "We're mammals, for one."

"You got that right, old son." Norbert looked off into a bramble of forsythia and poison ivy. He has an unusually expressive voice, one that I can listen to all day: a cross between Jimmy Stewart and Jon Stewart. "Among certain *other* commonalities."

Here we go, I thought.

He took a step forward into the light. "I wasn't going to mention it," he said, "but you've had a particularly lean and hungry look lately."

"Hey, I'm not saying I don't *like* meat."

"That would be a lie." He bent to slurp at an infection that oozed between the nails of his left paw. "It's written in the teeth, isn't it? The truth. Incisors up front for tearing, molars in the back for grinding."

I turned to dip my brush, and watched it fall the twelve feet to the plastic drop cloth with a clap that startled him. I clanked down the ladder to retrieve it.

"It's not a question of *preferences*," he said, followed by an exaggerated chomp-chomping sound.

"Well—" I wouldn't be drawn into a discussion of mammalian evolution with him, or anyone else for that matter. "I used my rational faculties. See, I can do that, Norbert. It's my prerogative as a rational being. I don't eat meat. Period. Because I choose not to. For ethical reasons we don't have to go into."

"Moving on."

"Anyway," I said, cleaning the brush bristles against the corner of the house. "So meat is what it's all about? For you?"

"Not just—" Norbert spotted a welling of pink light at the top of the maple tree. The sun would be cresting the eastern ridge soon. He turned to leave. "Keep it real."

"You know that I will."

I watched him slink across the lawn. Dazed and wide-eyed, the others in the pack raised their heads from the offices of their chewing, then scrambled after him. One little guy struggled with what was left of the carcass as far as the tree line along the back edge of my property before abandoning it there. Shoot, I was thinking, that'll draw turkey vultures for sure. I hate turkey vultures. But I'm too lazy to do anything about it. I hadn't showered yet, and there was an hour or so left before I had to leave for my real job.

* * *

The next morning Norbert didn't show, probably a good thing because my wife was up early. Belle is a small woman five years my senior. She's exceedingly intelligent, a genius even, though a little obsessive. She wonders aloud sometimes if I find her attractive anymore, because we're getting old, we're in our forties, and it's starting to show. I do find her attractive, still. That's not an issue. (We never discuss whether the converse is true.) Actually, to be frank, she's not just a little obsessive; she's OCD. It's clinical. She hails from a long, proud lineage of pink-handed oven checkers, window lockers, and oriental-rug-fringe-straighteners. She gets a lot of work done, though. She homeschools our son, and she's the pastor of our church, which she herself founded. I call it *our* church, though I'm not a strictly regular attendee. I haven't been to service since we embarked on the churchwide "group fast." It was supposed to last for three days, Good Friday to Easter morning. It was Belle's idea and everyone in the congregation—all thirty-seven members, even the ones who should have consulted their physicians—jumped right in. This included Belle herself and our son. On Easter morning, everyone gathered for Krispy Kreme doughnuts and testimony. Did the Lord speak? How? Did the Spirit move? Be specific. As I said, I wasn't there. The Lord had not spoken to me and never has, which has got to end sometime. So my fast continues, and the longer it goes on, the easier it seems to get. Belle doesn't know. She doesn't have to know everything about me, no matter how long we've been married. I have my own relationship with the Lord. And I've laid down the law. I won't eat again until He shows me some direction. In for a pound in for a penny. Plus, speaking of pounds—they're just falling away. I'm starting to look good in my jeans again. I can tuck my shirts in without feeling like an ungainly slob. I used to laugh at those cheesy weight-loss infomercials. The miraculous transformation. Not anymore.

Crouched in my wool socks, I was mixing the first coat of the color we'd selected, a deep bluish-gray called Thunderstorm, when Belle slipped out onto the deck without my knowing—and spooked me. "Can you go see what that is?" she said, pointing with her cup. As I stood up and looked, already knowing what she meant, she nestled in behind me, her chin on my shoulder and her arms out in front as though they were my own. "See it? Over there?" She set the mug down on the deck railing and pointed more precisely across our wide neatly cut lawn, aligning the axis of her arm and finger with my line of vision. Boots, the alcoholic landscaper, had been by the previous afternoon. I'm proud about how I've always kept up with the lawn.

"Yeah, I see it," I said.

Still inches from my ear, she tore into her morning Granny Smith and misted my neck with a spray of juice and spittle. I've arrived at a point in our marriage, in my life, when the most innocuous daily sounds, dependable morning sounds, can fill me with dread. The violent cacophony of Belle's apple chewing is one such sound. We've been married for seventeen years. "I'm aware of it, but thank you for the reminder."

"OK," she said, masticating, her mouth full. "I'll ask: What is it?"

"It's a deer's ribcage," I said.

She grimaced, vocally. "Well, can you throw it away?"

"Yes, dear," I said. "I *can* throw it away."

"Ah, but *will* you?" she said, pinging my neck, her thighs warm on the backs of my legs.

"Certainly. In the fullness of time."

"Won't it attract rats?" she asked. Rats and mold, rats and mold—she grew up in the Midwest, where people are preternaturally sensitive to the bitter fruits of neglect.

"Not rats," I said. "Something bigger."

* * *

A week later, forty-five minutes before dawn, I'm halfway through a second coat of Thunderstorm, multitasking again at the top of the ladder in my ruined boxers and damp wool socks. It's almost too cool to paint, but the latex is spreading well enough, and I'm nursing a thermos of coffee, just about all that I'll allow myself these days, and taking hits on a stale American Spirit. Belle considers smoking a defilement of the temple of the Holy Spirit. Nor am I allowed to smoke at work anymore, as per town ordinance, among other state statutes; we're long past the kidding and joshing stage. I've adjusted. I'm always adjusting. The last of a dying breed, I must be the only librarian in all of Christendom who hasn't quit. When I think of the unapologetic librarians of my youth, austere harridans all, with fury in their eyes and wormwood mockery on their lips, I'm astonished at how far we've degenerated from that lost tribe. *At their desks, they smoked.* The ones I remember probably drank there too. They were forces of nature, these women. They answered only to themselves. And we loved them for it.

I hear a rustle in the frost-stiffened underbrush along the edge of the woods, and Norbert and his posse appear, trotting Norbert in the lead, dripping with insouciance but alert in the shoulders, head up, ears erect. His home-dogs, the usual five or six, wrestle with something in their midst. I can't see what, exactly, but from the thrashing, it's obviously alive. I maneuver a turn on my ladder and call out,

"What do your gaunt fellows have today, Norbert?"

He sprints to the foot of the ladder and bounds up five or six rungs to nip at my ankles, his nails ringing on the aluminum as he clunks back down into the grass. "Whoa, now," I say.

"We were talking, last time, about *happy*." He's out of breath, his eyes bright. His tongue lolls and flashes. "About what makes me *happy*."

My heart squirms, the ladder vibrating beneath me. "Yeah, I remember." Just beyond the glow of the trouble lights, one of Norbert's pack members is dragging what I can clearly see now is a small deer by one of its bony joints. A fawn. A fawn is a baby deer.

"So I'm putting together a little demonstration." In a flash he's back among them. "Check this out," he says, ending in a howl. Their eyes on me, the crew is waiting on his word to sink their teeth in for real. I'm terrified and thrilled all at once and this only adds to my lightheadedness. A licit feeling courses through my chest; it's what I've imagined adultery feels like.

"Oh, man," I say. "Norbert, is this necessary?"

He gargles a laugh at me over his shoulder. "Is it *necessary*?" He translates for the others, who fall about snorting and yipping and flattening the grass with their backs. With the lapse of attention, the deer frees two of its legs, one front, one rear. But then the pack gathers itself, leaping to regain their bite holds on its trembling haunches. "You kill me, Gray."

"Well, what are friends for?" I take a hit on my cigarette to calm my nerves. "But can I be honest?"

"Wouldn't have it any other way, old son."

"I'm not 100 percent comfortable with this." Facing forward, I descend with my coffee, crablike, to the grass. "Is all I'm saying, buddy."

"Well, here's what *I'm* saying: be careful what you ask for." He mumbles something to the pack, then struts over to me, trying to keep his liquid spine and trembling musculature under control. "No, really, check this out." His breath clouds come fast as a choo-choo. His eyes shine, as does his coat. Molting season's over for Norbert. "I really think you're going to like this."

"What gives you that impression?"

"Because I got a feeling about you," he shoots back. As he sniffs the air between us, I take a sip of my coffee, trying not to shiver.

I cough unnecessarily. "Yeah? Why's that?"

"Come here," he says.

"No. Right where I am is fine."

He raises his eyebrows, or what pass for eyebrows on a coyote. "Just come over here for a minute."

All right. I think of the ur-librarians of the lost world, their brass balls, and steel myself. I step forward.

"*Closer,*" he says. He calls for the boys to bring up the captive fawn, which writhes piteously. "I've been thinking about you."

"Isn't *that* an ominous statement?"

"No, now. Just listen to me. I see this as a teaching opportunity."

I glance back at the house, the ladder, the paint can swaying from a hook I made from two wire coat hangers. The windows to my son's room are dark.

"I'm not going to ask you to get down on all fours or anything as trite as that. But you need to experience this up close. Let's move beyond *Animal Planet*."

"I don't even own a TV, Norbert."

"Sensitive, aren't we?" He smiles at the ground, then says something in Coyote, one of their names, which I'm surprised I recognize. The smallest dog, the one who's always eyeballing me from afar with his torn right orbital and yellow-fanged sneer, is glaring at me now over the fawn's spindly leg. "You ever hunt?" Norbert asks.

"Seriously. I don't eat meat. Am I going to hunt?"

"Anyway," he says, nonchalantly. He grumbles something, as though clearing his throat, and now they rush the fawn forward, right up against my knees and thighs. I can feel the heat of the fawn's short fur and these nodules or bumps that must be ticks gorging on its pink flesh beneath, and its breath is fetid, crazy-bad, and in the yellow light I can see its little pebbly teeth, which it bares as it snarls, eyes rolling. Past hope, the fawn itself is raging.

"Oh, God."

Norbert rears back like a cobra and buries his snout above its breastbone and the fawn explodes in an aerosol of gristle and blood. It's keening now, bellowing, screeching, a sound so far over the top, at first I laugh, and when I fall back against the ladder, something jangles and plummets to the grass behind me. I never even knew deer had vocal cords. And the noise coming of out Norbert is stranger still, half laugh, half howl. He's burbling with glee. Singing with the others as they feed. Like one being, rapt and joyous. He rears, scrambles over to me, and spits the animal's heart into the grass at my feet.

"Oh, wow," I say. I'm up against the foundation of my house, something wet on my elbow and calf, which I realize is spilled latex paint. "Breakfast, is it?" I laugh. "Norbert, you shouldn't have."

He lifts the heart in his mouth gingerly again, and circles the ladder to reach me. He mumbles something that I can't hear over my own uncontrollable giggling. He wants me to take the heart. I don't want to take the heart. He insists, his teeth bared, his eyes glistening, all pupil, all black. I take the heart.

"Big bite, now. That's all yours. Hurry. Big, big bite."

The organ snaps and twitches like something being born in my wet palm. To my astonishment, I'm flashing images from my Catholic youth—back before I was born again, and, to my horror, as in a dream—of the weeping Sacred Heart of Jesus.

"While it's still beating, Gray. Open up."

"It's not beating anymore."

"What! Just take a bite!"

"I can't—" I lift the heart to the environs of my face. It's about the size of a cherry tomato, and more than just heart; there's some bonus tissue around it, fatty and livid purple, and the splintered ends of jutting toothpick bones leaking marrow and lymph. I shake my head. "No—" But I do as Norbert asks. I grip it firmly with the fingers of both hands like a tiny hamburger, like a bite-sized slider from White Castle, and sink my front teeth down into the tissue, light-headed at the rush of old copper pennies (must all clichés turn out to be true in the end?) and gagging on fur and tainted milk and the pervasive smell-taste of shit. I try to wrench away a good-size chunk. At first it doesn't tear too good, but then it does, finally, stringily, and I'm left with a flap of warm convulsive muscle hanging halfway down my chin. My neck and chest are wet.

"Lord have mercy!" Norbert stands on his hind legs like some man dog, then levels out to spin in a tight circle three times, an anime mutt chasing its tail, paws stained with blood and blue-gray house paint. "Give me a howl, boy!"

Still gagging, I shake my head no.

"Swallow first, then give me good one!"

I swallow. The spastic flesh and bone scrape along the dark tunnel inside me. First solid food I've had in weeks. "Wooo," I howl, weakly, gagging.

"Louder, son!"

"Hooo!"

"With gusto!" he says. "Like you mean it!"

"I don't want to wake Belle," I manage to say.

Norbert ducks as though dodging a rolling pin, then comes back up all shoulders and guilty grimace. "Oh, Gray, I *completely* forgot. Give me the rest of that, will you? I assume you're finished?" I hold out what's left. He snaps it up, eyes to the skies, and swallows. "Too damn good to waste." And he's off. Halfway across the yard he slams on the brakes, scrambles back, and skids to a stop inches from my face, his damp eyes marbley, ecstatic. "*That's* what makes me happy."

I shield my head with my arms. "OK, good, I think I understand—"

"*Happy* doesn't quite cut it, does it, as a word?" He races off with the others. "*Words* don't cut it!" he howls one last time.

I catch my breath, struggled to my feet, leave everything where it is, and stagger inside to shower for work. As I scrape and peel my arms clean of the latex and rinse my hair, my tongue worries the stringy bits from my teeth, and bits of animal matter converge on the stainless steel drain filter. I hear my son stirring in his room.

At work, we're getting everything ready for the ribbon cutting. Structurally, the new library is complete, but the contractors are still hanging fabrics and laying bright fresh-napped blue carpet in the children's section. His honor the mayor will preside over the ceremony. A good conservative, my wife says. I've met the man, but I always feel invisible during encounters with big wigs like that. He has bad teeth and the worst toupee I've ever seen. Me, I have a lot of rich thick hair, graying but thick—CEO hair, Belle's brother once called it, laughing. I do like the mayor's ride, though: Lincoln Town Car, black, V-8, sweet chrome rims. I see him standing in supermarket checkout lines around town, blazer, open collar, and loafers, buying unidentifiable meats fresh from the butcher's hand. God bless the man for harnessing the political willpower, more than 10 million dollars' worth, for library expansion. The place is absolutely state of the art, straight from the pages of *Architectural Digest*.

Still, I can't get over the impression that there's something overcooked about it all. How everybody's gleeful to the point of delirium about the importance of books, yet most of the patrons come in for Internet access and free DVDs. And there's way too much open space, which I have to admit has done wonders for the *feng shui*, even in among the stacks. Maybe I should stop complaining; just because I kick it old-school doesn't mean the stacks have to be a foot and a half apart and housed in successively shorter basement levels until the lowest is just a dark crawlspace with a dirt floor.

I'm still feeling a little nauseated when I arrive. Despite a thorough oral irrigation with cherry Gatorade, I can't get the tang of fawn heart out of my throat, and I'm not looking forward to the hunk I swallowed's grand entrance into my intestines.

Margaret is tearing up the keyboard at the reference desk. She shops at vintage clothing stores, wears cat-eye glasses and Victorian-era ankle-length dresses the color of feral turkeys. And the bun: killer. Arousing, even. There's another secret, but who's counting: Belle knows nothing of my erotic cowpaths with regards to that particular hairstyle, how as a boy, balls cupped in my sweaty palms, I'd haunt the stacks, flush with imagining the heights to which I'd transport Ms. Allbritton or Mrs. Phaneuf, their buns fraying slowly into long airy strands as they rode my hips. So it's nice to come to work. Mostly. And easier here to hide my fasting, my ketone breath. Meetings and conference calls, I'm not so fond of, nor of the tension that arises from the pettiest of controversies. Like who gets the new Herman Miller chair.

When I'm out in Ann Arbor, they'll miss me.

"Yo, Margaret," I say, ducking into the staffroom. When I reemerge, I detect a ripple in her usually placid apprehension of her surroundings. "Boot up yet?" I ask. We're well into this new information retrieval system, too, the last library in the state to jettison its card catalogues. They're in my garage, the cards, in four wooden cabinets that weigh five hundred pounds each.

"Yeah, I'm fine," she says, so smooth and crisply articulate. She could record customer-service menus. "But I need your help with something."

"But of course." I take up a position behind her bun, catch a whiff of warm vanilla sugar shower gel.

"How do you save a Word document as a PDF file again?"

At least two dozen times I've shown Margaret, and everyone else in the library, how to save a Word document as a PDF file. This and how to modify one's screensaver delay. But the Lord counsels patience, and I've got nothing but time. In a flash, I'm manipulating Margaret's mouse even at this unlikely angle, pointing, clicking. PRINT AS—Voila. "Hey, you're a vegetarian, right?" I know this well enough by now, but I ask anyway. It's what Margaret and I do, this back and forth, like characters in a Beckett play.

"Oh, thanks, Grayson," she says. "Don't go away. Let me do it in front of you just to be sure." I linger as she lumbers through the motions. Then, in a tone saturated with her own long-suffering fatigue, she reminds me, once again, that, yes, she's a *vegan*. There's a difference.

Since beginning the fast, my eyes have been opened to the anorectic world around me—how, for instance, vegan status provides perfect cover for eating as little as one likes.

"Ever fall off the wagon?" I ask, still leaning on the desk.

She scratches at a fleck of paint on the back of my hand. "What's this?"

"Almost done with the paint job." I try not to think of how that felt, her sharp red nail on my flesh. "What happens when you do fall? Like, to your bowels?"

"Why are you asking?" she wonders aloud. "What a way to start the morning. What a question."

"I fell off the wagon." The official story at work is that I'm super picky about what I eat, for a man. "No big deal, though. I'm right back on it. The little vegetarian engine that could."

"No one's keeping score, you know."

So she thinks. I try to put it in a way she'll understand because she's a lapsed Buddhist, or some such thing. "It was sort of a moral dilemma, is what I was faced with. If offered food, even if it's meat, should not one partake rather than offend such an act of generosity?" It's the only thing I remember about the Buddha—that he once ate proffered lamb.

"What was it?"

"What did I eat?"

Paula minces by with a tart good-morning for the two of us. Head librarian, she's thin, but she suffers. I'd be surprised if she allows herself eight hundred calories a day.

"I don't want to disquiet you," I say.

"There's nothing you could say to disquiet me. Not at my age." Ms. Worldly Wise.

"Are we so jaded, Margaret?"

"Are we not adults, you and I?"

"I've known vegans who took things—viscerally. Like the time I consumed five pounds of raw ground chuck in front of one—a woman, a vegan." It's a lie. "To prove a point," I say. "Proved it, ran off, and vomited for an hour and a half. This was back in the day."

Margaret returns to typing, her eyes zombied by the flat-screen monitor. Her bun sits there like some delicious avant-garde onion.

"The heart of a fawn," I say. *Chew on that!*

She smiles out of one side of her face, an expression that epitomizes the five years we've worked together. She thinks she knows me so well. Like my wife.

"No, really. The still-beating heart. Could have been Bambi's."

"Really." She's clacking away.

"Al fresco, si."

Her bifocals have slid down to the tip of her nose. They look like Chekhov's pince-nez. Not altogether unsexy. "And what did *that* taste like?" All she needs is the bushy goatee.

"Hard to describe, really."

"Then why bother?"

"Fine: like a mouthful of antique pennies. There was a gaminess that had me gagging."

She looks at me over the glasses. We seem to have found the edge. "Where the hell *were* you?"

"My backyard. Before work."

Paula scissors back through. "What are we on now?"

"Grayson ate raw deer heart this morning in his backyard."

Paula stops. "Oh, deer heart!" she says, fixing me in her inscrutable gaze. She's in her late fifties and dresses in softly draped earth tones and immaculate textures. "Did you have to send away for that? To Omaha? My uncle enjoys all that stuff."

"No, this was fresh meat." Suddenly, the moment begins to open out. The lightheadedness is back. They're looking at me, waiting for something, but I'm over wide water. Wide, wide water.

"*How* fresh?" Paula asks, her expression dithering. She's a super-intelligent person who hates to be the one on the outside of the joke. I can understand that. Sometimes I can be so hard to read.

"Beating," I say. "Twitching."

"So how was that?" she asks. "Something you'd recommend?"

"I've had better."

"And Belle?" she asks. "Where was Belle during all this?" Belle is a sensitive topic at work. Her growing local renown as an evangelical minister is. Come to think of it, these women have *never* known how to read me. We're from separate worlds.

Sleeping, I tell them. The silence drags on, the room telescoping silently in and out. "Hey, I don't know what you guys would have done, but it was offered, and I accepted. Simple as that. Hospitality is, like, sacred, right? Or where would it end? I don't even want to think about that."

I watch them watching me. They're waiting for me to puncture the tension. To bring it all down around us. *Ha, ha! That Grayson!* I let them wait.

* * *

Tonight, after helping my son with a project on the misleading stages of embryonic development ("Ontogeny recapitulates phylogeny"? In a pig's eye!) and tucking him in, I slip into my own bed. Belle is asleep. She stirs at the displacement of the mattress, whispers something I can't understand, then falls back to snapping and chomping in her sleep. I nestle in behind her, into a wedge of comfort and warmth, set my hands free to graze and roam a little. That's when I hear the call of the wild. Responding, she stirs again but doesn't surface. My mind drifts to thoughts of Norbert taking care of business himself somewhere out there. He must have his own companion, though he's never mentioned one. I read somewhere that coyotes are monogamous. But does Norbert ever play around on the side? Belle trundles toward me. I slide down in the sheets to take one of her nipples in my mouth as half-asleep she holds me absently to her chest. These furtive dispensations of middle age, these embers.

Hearing something just outside, under the window, I'm reminded of my disquieting breakfast, the mouth feel—one of Belle's favorite cooking terms—and I bail out with a barrel roll as though parachuting into occupied territory. My wife retrogrades into sleep. My mouth wide and drying now, I listen for a crunching underfoot in the crushed stone along the house's eastward wall. And there it is. Unmistakable. I shuffle to the blinds and part them to look down into the purplish murk, strips of shadow where the streetlight can't touch. He's there, I know it, hard to define, but there nonetheless, curled in the grass, hungry, his fur swelling with every breath. All's right with the world, isn't it, Norbert? Tomorrow makes four weeks without solid food. Even so, my own heart continues to do its thing. Back in bed, I plunge headlong into the dreamless sleep of the faithful.

* * *

Saturday morning, just before dawn.

I'm replacing the crosshatch lattice around the base of the deck. The old lattice has been gnawed by small animals, which like to hole up under there and cause problems when they die. I'm absurdly proud of myself, having successfully measured and cut the pieces, as well as the molding to run the length of its edges. The sky is bright enough without the trouble lights, and I have all the time in the world. Belle and my son are in Stamford for two days, at a conference for homeschoolers; Belle's chairing a panel on biology curricula. So I don't have to pretend to eat a thing. I'm sitting in the Adirondack chair with a kitchen drawer in my lap, trying to find the chuck key to my old power drill, and sipping lukewarm bouillon, which I allow myself from time to time, when I hear the crisp snap of a twig. Norbert appears at the edge of the woods, in midsentence: "Now don't get your back up when I say this." Here he comes, alone, with jaunty gait.

"Norbert, what's up?" I'm wondering where his boys are, his crew. I'm afraid to ask. He looks a little crazed around the eyes. This is the latest I've ever seen him; it's nearly full daylight. He's got something in his mouth. What, I don't know, until he walks right up to lie in the grass next to the Adirondack. It's all I can do to keep still as the fleas begin to alight on my bare legs.

"I had a thought," he says.

I'm trying to remember the common wisdom about daytime

sightings of nocturnal creatures. Do they *always* have rabies? "What are you eating there, Norbert?"

"What if you adopted me?"

When I realize he's been feeding on hedgehog, I gag, broth laving my adenoids. Some of it drips into the kitchen drawer. Norbert is oblivious.

"We're onto that again?" I manage.

"Look, it'll be easy. We'll work it all out ahead of time. You come home from work one day and you've got me in a collar, on a leash, looking all docile."

He sounds serious.

"We'll get me bathed and my nails clipped. Snap. No one's going to know."

I imagine my hand stroking his fur, my fingers running along his spine. "So you're assuming I'm not going to move to Ann Arbor."

"Be serious," he says. "You're not going anywhere."

"That's the kind of encouragement I'm always aching for." Amazingly, I find the chuck key. "Bingo," I say, happy to have something to do with my hands. I lay the drawer down and gather up my drill and the box of bits and sit back down to loosen the chuck.

"I'm surprised you don't have a dog already."

"I can't see myself scooping poop," I say, tightening the chuck down onto a drill bit. "I see these people. It's like, who's the master?"

"Is that all that's bugging you? Get what's-his-name to do it."

"*What's-his-name?*"

Norbert stops chewing, a touch of panic in his eyes.

"You mean my son?" I ask.

"Yeah. Sorry. What *is* his name?"

"Norbert, it's Paul. Apple of my eye. Write it down."

"The look on Paul's face—think of that. Every boy needs a dog. Tell them you picked me up at the pound. That it was a rescue-dog type situation. Tell them they were going to put me down. Say it just like that: 'They were going to *put him down*.'"

"You mean lie?" I say. I shake my head. "My life is half over— more than half over. No more lying."

"You know what the life expectancy of a coyote is out here? I'm a goner. You wouldn't be lying, Gray."

"What breed would I say you are?"

"Look it up. You're a librarian. Tell them I'm a mutt. Say my father was half borzoi, half Rhodesian ridgeback, and my mother was a dingo. Be specific. That always works better."

"Right. Belle would be thrilled."

"Would she even notice?" He catches my eye from the corner of his. "Hey, be a pal and scratch my back."

I don't say anything, just cock my head.

"Sorry," he says. "Is that too much to ask?"

As I lower my hand into his bony fur, my bare forearm comes alive. The fleas settle like bits of black ash. I want to pull away. "What about the rest of the pack?"

"That's their tough luck."

I continue to root with my fingernails in his gritty flesh, the fleas feasting now.

He raises his head from the rancid hedgehog and looks around. "I'm basically a yard dog."

"Think you'd actually enjoy dog food?" Finally, I ease my hand away. "It's pretty foul."

"You'd hook me up with something fresher," he says. "Right?"

"You mean like beef?"

"Beef, lamb, chicken. Beef would be fine. I'm done with deer and this—" With his paw he nudges the hedgehog carcass away.

I get up and walk over to the deck. Norbert follows, his tongue working over a strip of fur that's snarled in his teeth. I plug the drill into the end of an orange extension wire I draped out of the bathroom window, and test the connection. The drill whines to life—once, twice.

"You still a vegetarian?" he says, standing a few feet away. "Or is that over?"

Not even Norbert knows about my ongoing fast. That's between me and Jesus. "What about Wednesday?" I ask.

"That was a gift. Me to you. From the heart."

"Hardy-har-har."

Norbert grins with mock shame. Down on one knee, I position the molding against the corner post of the deck. I need another hand to hold it in place while I drive the first screw.

"I could see it in your face. You weren't exactly crazy about it."

"Want the truth?" I ask. "It was way gamey."

"Sing it, brother. Yes. You see what I'm saying, then? Do I not, too, deserve the spice of variety?"

"Let me sleep on it."

"While they're away, just wash me down, a little shampoo wouldn't hurt. You got a hair dryer?"

Something washes over me; Jesus comes through. What am I doing sitting here talking to a goddamn coyote? That's not normal. "Can you hold this for me?"

Norbert lowers his snout to pin the molding in place with the flat of his forehead. "You got nail clippers?" he says to the grass.

That's how it is with me! Sometimes it can take a while. *Well, thank you, Jesus!* is what I want to say. But I'm feeling a little dizzy.

"Well, then, pick some up tonight," he says. "They're coming home, what, tomorrow?"

"Mmm-hmm."

"So, then, tomorrow. Let's go for it."

"We shall see." I swap out the drill bit for a Phillips head driver bit, slip a screw onto the tip, then lean in as I power up the old drill.

"I could return the favor."

"That's good," I say, happy to drown out the sound of his voice with whine of the drill. "You can step back now."

"You could run with us, at night," he says. "I think you'd enjoy it. What am I talking about? I *know* you would."

Lining up another screw, I imagine myself down on all fours trying to keep up. I've had a taste, so to speak. "You do know that my wife's a minister, with all that that entails."

"Well, jeez, not *every* night, Gray. I know how it is. Just on a weekend here and there? After the family's asleep." He yawns. "Do you need me to hold anything more with my head?"

"No, I'm good."

"This would be our little thing."

When I ask him where this is all coming from, he ignores the question. It's disingenuous of me anyway, because I know where it's all coming from, and, if I'm honest with myself, where it's all going.

"One-hand-washes-the-other type thing," Norbert says, squinting into the full morning light. A chill rattles out from my damp shoulder blades: I've never seen him like this, sunlit. I read somewhere that eastern coyotes have been interbreeding with Canadian wolves. That's why they're larger here than out west. "You hear what I'm saying?"

"The only thing is—" I line up another screw. "You don't have hands."

He tries to hold back a sneer, but he can't. He moves closer.

When I reach for another screw, I feel the rough dry rasp of his tongue on my wrist and yank it back as though scalded.

"What do you say?"

★ ★ ★

Tonight, in bed, alone, my anxiety seems to break loose and emerge into the world a living thing. My heart stirs like crossed wings, and I arise. The lightheadedness is worse now. I concentrate on my breathing. Belle has the kind of faith that leads her to lay hands on someone with pancreatic cancer, then await measurable results. She's in the world but never of it. "The doctors don't know our Jesus," she says. And I don't disagree: He is a personal God. But for me this just means you can't get to him any other way. And I remind myself that whatever manifestations are to come will not come as columns of fire or salt pillars. No fireworks, not for adults, not in this age. "When it comes," Belle has said, "it won't need interpretation." I wish I could agree with that.

I hear a gritty rustling in the gravel under the window. Like an elderly man, slumped and tentative, I sock-slide to the venetian blinds and part them to look down into the shadow there. No moon tonight. Even the corner streetlamp is dark. Then I realize the power is out, not just in my house but up and down the street. I slide out of the room and along the hallway to the cellar door, descend into a realm of mold. If Norbert's out there, he need only lower his head to the window well to see into the cellar. Carefully, I run my hand along the top of the cement wall just past where the joists end. Years before, we had rats. (Belle's fears are never completely unfounded.) A woman exterminator laid down a line of poison packets, two of which I later found chewed open by teeth the size of rice; the remaining packets I left intact where they were, insurance against future infestations. When I find one, damp and wilting, I lift it down like something radioactive or sacred.

Upstairs, after I catch my breath, I pull two filet mignon medallions from the refrigerator's lower drawer. They're for an anniversary meal later in the week, but I'm betting Belle forgot all about them. I strip the medallions from their flimsy shrink wrap, then lave them like plump fetuses in a stream of tepid tap water. With a paring knife I open a slit, from the side, then push deep with my index finger into the red core of their thickness—one, then the other. In the dark, I shake the rat poison like a packet of Sweet'n Low, tear it open, tap out a line of white grains into the pursed wound in the meat, pinch it tightly shut like thin lips, repeat, then wrap the filets in foil and slip them into the fridge.

Back in bed now and lighter than a soap bubble. I give my fingers a cautionary sniff, trying to decide what I detect on them, poison or the beef? I resist the urge to lick. I drift. Sometime after midnight, with the crunch of gravel beneath my window, I'm startled awake several times, afraid that Norbert can somehow see into the depths of my dark plan. The power has returned.

The next morning, before dawn, I emerge into the blue dampness of the deck to await the arrival of Norbert and his boys along the edge of the woods, but he's already curled in the shadows, up against the new lattice that rings the deck, and when I lean on the railing, he says, in a level voice, simply, "Grayson."

"Norbert," I say, pulling back. I take a long controlled breath. I feel ancient. "Where is everyone else?"

He snorts. "Who cares?" I follow the sound of his breathing along the side and around the corner of the deck to the foot of the stairs, where he appears, grainy and insubstantial. Do I run and get the filets now? I should have carried them out to begin with. *Steady me, Jesus. See me through this.* "It's just me this morning," he says, yawning, his ears stretched back, his saliva snapping.

"Good enough." But I'm hardly aware of what I'm saying. My mouth is numb. How deep in am I? Will the pack avenge his death? Will they ever know? I imagine Norbert gagging on the meat in a circle of confusion, coyotes running here and there. Rat poison is a desiccant that leaves one unable to drink enough water. A death by thirst.

"You said you'd sleep on it. Have you slept on it?"

"I have a little treat for you," I say, trying to pace myself.

Norbert floats up from the murk at the bottom of the deck stairs. "A treat," he says flatly. "You have a treat for me."

"I was cleaning the freezer last night." It's an unnecessary lie. "Yes, a treat."

"I can't say I'm not intrigued."

"Yeah, well, I thought, why not give Norbert a little taste? Maybe it's not all it's cracked up to be. This idea of his."

My ears seem stuffed with silence. I'm praying, *Jesus, see me through.* I'm so hungry myself. *Jesus, do right by me.* But the words that seem to struggle into consciousness—*thy will be done*—these I ignore.

Norbert fades into the shadow, just his snout visible, then seems to well forward again. "I gotta level with you, Gray, you don't sound—well."

"Norbert, you want the meat or not?" I ask. "They're, like, twenty-one bucks apiece. Belle bought them."

"I'm coming up." But after the first step, he hesitates. He can see into me now, I'm sure. He knows the contours of my soul.

"Let me bring them out."

"Aren't you eating with me?"

I smile. It's thin and unconvincing. "I told you, Norbert. I'm a vegetarian."

"Bullshit."

"Excuse me?"

"That's bullshit," he repeats. "What about Wednesday? And since when does a vegetarian keep filet mignon around the house?"

"OK, let's cut the crap. You want to come in? Is that where we're going with this? Just say it." I slide open the glass door and stand aside. "Knock yourself out."

"You don't have to be like that, Gray." Norbert takes a few cautious steps forward, head low. "But as long as you're asking—"

I watch him cross the threshold, his nails raking the floor tile. And it hits me: *Jesus Christ, there's a coyote in my kitchen.* I step inside and pull the sliding glass shut behind me. Over near the dishwasher, Norbert's eyes shine in the blue-green glow of the nightlight. Except for our breathing and the ticking of the plastic clock above the sink, the house is quiet while out in my backyard, in the darkness, a dozen eyes drift and hover, blazing with orange retinal shimmer.

ORCHARD TENDER

A week before the owner of the orchard died, Larry whistled for me above the rumble of the tractor, and I lowered myself from the tree I'd been pruning and walked to where he stood with his arms crossed in the grassy margins of the orchard, where we dumped branches and grass cuttings. The fawn hadn't been there more than a day. Its brown-red hide had been torn back like the skin of a vinyl couch, its organs still slick as eels. In July the carcass would have been thick with flies, but here we were in February.

Larry told me to throw it into the woods. He always initiated such requests with the phrase *Let me make a suggestion.* He was about fifty years old and had thick, cracked hands. The small finger of one of them was just a stub he screwed a gold wedding band down onto every morning, even though he hadn't seen his wife in twenty years. He never wore gloves, no matter how cold. "No big deal," he said, toeing the animal's hoof and sucking at his teeth, his voice, as always, level and dry. I'd worked with him for five summers and for five winter breaks, so I thought I knew how to interpret what was in his eyes. But it was like reading the names on worn gravestones in the cemeteries that lay scattered throughout the countryside. His discovery bothered him; that much was clear. The way the deer's long head flopped over when I lifted it, the blackness of its eye, its tongue pink between dry black rubbery lips.

"Coyote did this," Larry said.

"In Connecticut?" I still knew how to give good son back then. I was twenty-four, young enough to be the illegitimate child of one of the many encounters with women Larry no longer bothered to brag about. The idea seemed ludicrous to me, though, that he might be related to anyone other than himself.

"They're reclaiming their old territory." He climbed onto the tractor. "Moving back in from the north."

"You've seen them?"

He put the tractor in gear and drove away, his shoulders bouncing with the dust.

I crouched to marvel at the fawn's short hair and weird soft ears. Then I dragged the thing by one of its hooves for a few yards, its head catching in the brambles. When I tried lifting it, the insides didn't ooze out, because they were frozen. I started spinning. I had the thing by the legs, my boots doing a tight little dance. When I let it go, one of my gloves went with it, and I almost fell back, the corpse snapping in the underbrush as it came to rest. Out in the orchard again, I found my hand shears and climbed back into the tree. For the rest of the day I was on edge, keeping off the ground longer than necessary, lingering over the view. Listening for a sign.

During August in the orchard, the world was moist and spiraled out green and ripe from your mount in the flat crowns of the trees. You watched cloud shadows slide over distant hills. In the rain it didn't matter; you just stayed up there, even though the owner didn't require it, because the water rinsed the powdered pesticides from the crannies in your skin. The summer before, I'd been up there pruning with Larry, balancing in a tree of Fuji apples adjacent to his, when out of nowhere he said, "Yeah, well, I like you." As though we'd been having a discussion all along. As though we talked every day, like two normal guys who worked together.

I waited until I was sure of the evenness in my voice. "And why's that, Larry?"

He didn't pause in his work. He didn't look at me. It was like a window opening, but only for a moment. "You're not afraid of being alone."

I wasn't sure what to say.

"That's rare." He let a sucker fall to the grass, fat end first, the leaves shedding their dusty coating of pesticide on impact. "It's good practice, too."

We'd continued working in silence, surrounded by the dense greens of late summer.

But here, now, in February, everything, not just the deer, seemed dead. Below me, the edge of the woods kept pulling my eyes, and I waited for the insouciant lope I associated with all things feral, with dingoes and wolves, tongues tasting the air, heads riding low between their shoulders.

After sunset and a few beers, I rode my ten-speed back to the orchard, and searched the underbrush with a flashlight shaped like a fat yellow pistol. The woods were brittle-cold and quiet, the upper limbs rasping in the breeze. I found the deer carcass and, after listening to the darkness for a moment, sat cross-legged with my sketch pad and the warm light in the crook of my neck. The animal's left hind leg was hung up in a wrist-thick hanging vine, its face folded under its torn chest as though shying from me. I sketched it as-is. New material, something I hungered for. I'd painted the Simms factory at the edge of town too many times, its arched windows broken and dark for years now. On Sundays in June and July, I'd ride out after work and set up my homemade easel in the gravel parking lot, fascinated by the play of shadows on the red bricks as they faded to pink and orange in the last light. It was an expensive hobby, and I didn't make much. I cut corners by stretching my own canvas over scraps of wood from the orchard, but oil paints weren't cheap. If I could have phrased it correctly, the power those dead walls had, I would have given up trying to paint them: a sort of hardness born of sunlight and texture of red brick, the shadows lengthening. My grandmother, who'd died when I was a child—I'd never known her—had worked a loom between those walls for decades. It wasn't an unpleasant feeling, this desolation—that's what troubled me. Tonight I sat in a cone of moist calm with my dead fawn and the thought of coyotes out there prowling, picking up the scent of rotting meat, circling in.

The next morning I found Larry at his usual spot before work: sitting on the lowered gate of the old Roadmaster station wagon the owner let him drive. He was gnawing an unripe peach and wearing the same dark mustard insulated overalls he'd worn since the day I first shook hands with him. All February, we'd been pruning. I'd been in the trees, snipping and dropping shoots. My wrists and forearms were ropy with sinew. Larry had gathered up the branches, loaded them on the wooden flatbed trailer, and driven them to the corners of the orchard to dump. The owner left the details to Larry, who'd worked the orchard for twenty-nine years, earning his wages since day 1 under the table, without a contract or health insurance or a pension. Larry lived in a dented 1954 Airstream, another perk. It sagged on flat tires out of sight of the road. The silver plating had cracked and curled, and often, during his dealings with the owner, I'd see Larry lean against it absently peeling away large patches of foil-like chrome. He and the owner knew the contours of their relationship so well, what it would and would not consist of, that it seemed they barely spoke. From afar—I always left them alone—the owner communicated with hand signals, pointing this way and that, making zipping motions, chopping motions, all of it unnecessary, because Larry knew what needed to be done before the owner did, knew the orchard better than anyone, every inch of it, so the signals themselves were like the signs a third-base coach flashes a veteran batter. I brought it up once in the barn, and Larry hawked and spit and said I ought to be thankful he'd spared me the sound of a boss's voice. "You just don't know how lucky you are," he said. "You'll learn."

* * *

As far as we knew the owner had been in northern California. He never went into much detail about his travels, which were rare. On a Thursday at about two o'clock, Larry was leaning against the trunk of an Idared tree that I was pruning. That morning I'd scraped a knuckle, and it was still bleeding. He gave me his signal whistle, an annoying *whip-poor-will*. "Company," he said. "Look there."

"Anyone you know?"

He shook his head. "Suits." Like a synonym for the clap, the way he said it. He'd been cleaning his fingernails with the broken blade of his jackknife. He took his time folding it up and slipping it into his pocket.

I lowered myself through the bare branches, and together we watched a black Mercedes sedan with Rhode Island license plates slow to a stop just inside the wrought-iron archway at the entrance to the fields. Two slender men in identical camelhair overcoats got out and stood on either side of the car.

"I knew it," said Larry.

One of them wore wraparound sunglasses that glinted in the afternoon sun. "You Gary?" he called to us. Larry didn't move, his hands at his sides, ready. I could see they were trembling, but his voice revealed nothing.

"Who wants to know?"

"Your boss died."

"And?" he said, after a pause.

"Out in San Fran. Heart attack." The lawyer came around the front of the car and stood with his hands crossed in front of him, a vaguely military posture. He wore expensive leather gloves and narrow leather wingtips with thin soles.

Larry continued to stare the men down.

"All right," the lawyer said, "here's what you're going to do: just keep working until the estate is settled."

"He said that?"

"I'm saying it." The lawyer bared his teeth and tightened his gloves. "I just told you. He's dead."

The other lawyer was shorter and younger, with more hair. He was probably just out of law school. "You just keep doing what you're doing, and we'll let you know when to stop. We'll send word."

"It took two guys to deliver that message?"

The first lawyer scratched his neck and checked his watch. "Right. Any questions?"

Larry scooped an armful of suckers and heaved them onto the trailer. "If something comes up, I'll have my lawyer drop you a line."

The younger one pointed at me and said, "How about you?"

I shot Larry a glance, making sure he was listening. "Where'd you get those shoes?"

Larry gave me a constipated look. "That's enough."

The lawyer with the sunglasses surmised the property, chin raised. "The sister's coming up from Tampa." He took in the house and the barn, the long line of chicken coops and the array of dilapidated machinery in the shadow of the oak tree. He was glad not to be us. "She'll square things away."

"The sister," said Larry. "Got it."

Though I knew next to nothing about the owner, it didn't seem possible that he could have a sister. He was more of a force of nature, as inevitable as the rain or the passing cumuli.

The lawyers glanced at one other with mild annoyance and got in the car. It had been running all along but was too expensive to hear. We watched it back out of the gravel drive, through the iron archway—the film of their advent running in reverse now—and pull silently onto the asphalt. The lawyers smiled and shook their heads behind the tinted windows as they drove away.

Larry busied himself. "So."

"I don't believe it."

"What is it you don't believe?" He paused to look at me. "Time is passing. Surprise."

"Jesus," I said. "I don't believe it."

Larry put his hands on his hips. "Let me make a suggestion."

* * *

Two months passed. My head down, I worked on into a silence that seemed to mount with the days. Nothing else seemed to change. Larry and I pruned, endlessly. We went back over the rows of Empires and Cortlands and Red Delicious again and again until it became impossible to maintain the fiction we were doing useful work. The orchard was pruned out, the trees more streamlined than they'd ever been. Perfect. So I mended wooden apple crates. I stacked them in rows ten high, more wooden crates than anyone could ever use. Work for work's sake. Fine with me. Larry removed the blade from each of the mowers, in service or scrap, and sharpened it manually, the hollow scrape of metal on whetstone issuing from the recesses of the barn, and laid each shining blade on the greasy workbench. He grew even quieter than usual. Weeks passed without a word. He began to break the engines down, examining pistons and cranks for wear, rinsing everything in a tray of oily gasoline, drying and putting aside parts that might require replacement. The sharp tang of petroleum eddied in his wake whenever he passed. Every fourteen days, our checks appeared in the orchard mailbox, signed by the CFO of a law firm in Providence.

In April, when we'd usually begin our weekly mowing of the orchard grass, another car appeared. I'd just driven the tractor into the maw of the barn and cut the ignition. In the delicious silence, I heard tires crunching the gravel driveway of the owner's house. Larry was off somewhere in the orchard. He'd been disappearing for whole days at a time without explanation, reappearing, whenever he did, without warning. I knew better than to say anything. I was fine with it—the solitude. That's what I called it in my mind.

Out of the barn in the afternoon sun, I saw two women stretching their arms and legs near a black Volvo station wagon with Florida license plates. "Hello," said the older of the two, a bit startled when she finally saw me. She was trim, tan, leathery, her neck skin taut; handsome, you might say—I'd never known how well the word could apply to a woman—and in good shape for someone who looked to be in her mid-fifties. Confident in a way I associated with time spent on expensive boats sipping cocktails with sexually suggestive names. "Are you Larry?" she asked.

"No," I said wiping my hands on my greasy jeans. "Larry's out in the orchard."

"I don't know who you are." She was looking past me at the barn, the diesel pump, the cracked filthy windows of the greenhouse. "What's your name?"

I told her.

"OK, well, I'm Lillian." She smiled thinly, her eyebrows penciled half-circles. "Would you be a champ and help us with our luggage?"

Before she could finish, I'd walked around to the back of the car, past the younger of the two women, a girl, really, and was opening the hatch.

"June's in a poor mood," she said. "June is pouting. Say hi, June."

June paid me no mind. I began lugging their bags up the walkway to the house, returning several times for more. These people didn't travel light. June gave no indication I was even there. She was wandering around the yard, throwing her arms out in mock-rapture. At first, watching covertly, I felt embarrassed for her. She looked about seventeen or so. She wore loose Day-Glo orange shorts that showed off her paste-white thighs, a turquoise halter sweater I found myself growing fonder of with each return trip to the car.

"Oh, I just *love* it," she said, addressing the breeze and the rows of apple and peach trees and the very air. Who was she performing for? I'd been invisible to girls her age for some time. Maybe forever. Lillian ignored her daughter for as long as she could, but then she stopped short on the walkway.

"We'll be here for a while," she said. "So knock it off."

"No, but I *love* it."

"You wanted to come." Lillian was fishing in her purse. "You didn't have to come."

I realized with horror what she was doing. "That's not necessary."

"No, no," Lillian said. "I don't expect you to—"

I was already walking away with my hands in my pockets.

* * *

From the bucket of the cherry picker, I thinned peaches and watched June sunbathe on the south-facing slopes of the orchard, the straps of her lime-green, one-piece bathing suit loose as she lay on her stomach, her breasts bulging visibly white on each side. Though this went on for weeks, she seemed unaware of my fascination. Whenever she did notice me, I'd wave or nod, as professionally detached an acknowledgment as I could muster. I knew how to play the roles well: Manual laborer. Orchard tender. Background worker. On my trips to the orchard after dark to sketch my dead deer, I began lingering in the deep shadows of the barn with a set of binoculars the owner had years before left hanging from a nail. Those windy nights, the corner window of June's room seemed to float above me as though the darkness itself were a wall you might look through. But the blinds never opened. I never caught more than a hint of shifting form or color beyond the horizontal slats. To be ashamed of yourself, you need a self. You need to be someone. Watching through those binoculars for hours, waiting for the rectangle of whiskey-tinted cream to go black, I was nothing but a pair of eyes. As invisible as the gulf of air above me. Navigating the roads home each night, I resolved to go straight to the fawn the next evening, but I knew this was nonsense. I'd be back in the shadows of the barn twenty-four hours later.

One night the binoculars were gone. I crept out of the barn and lay in the dry grass listening for a sign of movement. For hours there was only the rub and rattle of the broken weathervane to texture the silence.

The next morning Larry sat on the lowered gate of the station wagon, its wheels almost completely lost in clouds of Queen Anne's lace. I hadn't seen him in two weeks. He'd shaved his head. His scalp was pocked and sunburned, his eyes red-rimmed. The binoculars hung from his neck on their frayed leather strap. "She's an eyeful," he said, smiling to himself as I passed. "Yessir."

I was wheeling my bicycle toward the barn. I stopped. "Excuse me?"

"I said, she's a looker. Easy on the eyes."

"I'm going to give the northeast corner another pass today with the mower." The grass in the northeast corner, like the grass in every corner of the orchard, would not need mowing for a week. Grass didn't grow that quickly. We weren't dealing with putting greens.

"You go right ahead." Larry swung his legs from the gate of the station wagon. "As long as that money's coming in, might as well make yourself useful. If you ask me it's a matter of self-respect. Like so much else."

"Don't talk about her that way."

"Don't talk about who that way?"

"Let's cut the crap," I said. "You know who I mean."

Larry scratched his white whiskers with the stump of his finger. I'd never seen him go so long without a shave. He looked like some weathered wise man. He smiled and squinted. "Oh, no, no, I was talking about Lillian." He pointed his chin past me.

Here came Lillian across the gravel driveway carrying an enormous jar of pickles in both hands. "Gentlemen," she said, presenting the jar as though it were some supreme test, "help me out, will you." What would we idiots do? Larry nudged past me to take the pickles from her. But Lillian recoiled from him. Embarrassed, she handed the jar to me. I managed to loosen the lid. She thanked us and started for the house, her narrow well-kept haunches mincing efficiently.

Larry slipped the binoculars from his neck. "Here," he said, still squinting. "I know you'll get much more use out of them than I would."

"Knock it off," I said, taking them.

Here Lillian came again, walking much more quickly this time. She paused some distance from us with her wrist cocked on her jutting hip. "Just to clarify where we stand at the moment," she said, "because we haven't really had the chance to articulate anything long-term." She explained that she had, as we might have guessed, "no real interest" in maintaining an orchard, so, sadly, this year's crop would be the last. She didn't seem very sad. She and June would be leaving before the end of the summer. The orchard had been listed with a local realty. After the harvest, there'd be a modest severance payment for both of us. She didn't know how much yet, but it was the least she could do, her brother would have wanted it that way. The trees would be cleared. The land would be graded and subdivided. The lots would be sold for residential housing. That's what she did down in Florida. She was a realtor. I imagined her standing at the edge of the Everglades in khakis and a hardhat, a rolled set of blueprints in her fist. She'd even offered a tentative title for the properties: Applewood Estates.

Without thinking, I looked at Larry.

"I like it," he said, his eyes moist and bright.

Lillian did that thing with her mouth that passed for smiling. "Well, then," she said after a moment. We were to stay focused, we were to maximize the harvest, we were to keep on keeping on. As events warranted, she would "touch base." She lifted the lid-loosened jar. "Thank you again, gentlemen."

"Thank *you*," Larry said. He watched her walk away. Then, avoiding my eyes, he raised the gate of the station wagon and pressed it shut. I heard the screen door of the Airstream clap twice.

That morning I lingered in the barn pretending to fill the gas tank of the mower and fiddling with the oil cap, willing June to appear. Finally, after an hour, I felt I must commit to starting the engine and to driving off into the orchard. I did so. As I swung the mower into the row of Granny Smiths that had always offered the best view of her usual sunbathing spot, there she was, lying on her side on a huge beach towel, her head propped on her elbow, reading. I let up on the throttle, and the mower rattled in neutral beneath me. I looked around for Larry. I cut the engine, climbed off into the sudden silence, my heart racing, and crossed a row of Lodis, their branches already heavy with yellow-green fruit, then two rows of immature peaches. "Excuse me," I said, too softly. She gave no indication she'd heard me. Then louder: "Hi."

She startled. "Oh, God, you scared me."

I apologized, mindful to keep the distance between us. I asked what she was reading; and when she told me, her voice laced with fatigue and annoyance, I nodded as though I'd heard of the author. "You seem pretty bored," I said.

"Well, *yeah*." She held up the book.

I reached for a branch of peaches in the tree above me and fell to thinning a few from the dense clump. The peaches didn't need to be thinned. The clumps were thin enough. "There's a bar in town, you know."

She looked at me over the book. "And?"

"Just a dive, but—"

"You're not doing what I think you're doing," she said, the

curve of her hip accentuated beautifully by how she lay. "What's your name again?"

I told her again. "What do you think I'm doing?"

"Asking me out."

I tossed a hard peach into the distance. At the far end of the row, Larry sauntered past with an antique scythe. He paused when he caught sight of me, the blade over his shoulder, then continued on.

"How *old* are you?" she asked.

"I'm in college." Technically that was no longer true. I wasn't going back in the fall. I owed the university money. I had none. "Jesus, how the hell *old* do I look?"

"Don't get your shorts in a bunch." She sat up. "I'm just asking. I can't ask?"

"How old do I look?" I asked again.

"I don't know. I don't want to say." She looked down the row of trees and spotted Larry wandering with the scythe. "How old is *that* guy?" she asked, fussing behind her neck with the strings of her bathing suit.

"Fifty or thereabouts," I said. I held up my hands. "Hey, never mind."

"*Never mind* what?"

"About that bar and whatnot."

"You *sound* old," she said. "Who says *whatnot?* Who says *thereabouts?*"

"Well." I gave her a corny salute and turned to leave. "Thanks for your consideration."

"So, you draw?" she asked.

I turned back. "When I can find the time."

"I'm not saying no about the bar and whatnot." She lay on

her stomach again and opened the book. "Not that I'm technically old enough to drink."

"You don't drink?"

"Bye," she said.

Back at the barn, as I switched off the tractor's ignition, Larry materialized from a small room that had once served as an office. He held the scythe in one hand, the whetstone in the other. "Backdoor man," he mumbled. "Hoochie coochie man."

I walked to the red refrigerator I stored my beer in. Beneath the rust you could still make out the Coca Cola insignia, the words ICE COLD. The thing hummed and vibrated. Larry spat on the whetstone and shuffled out squinting into the bright sunlight.

Later, when I heard the screen door of the owner's house, I stood beer in hand to press my face against a crack in the barn's withered boards. Lillian walked to the Volvo, her cadence smart and confident. She got in and drove off. I finished the beer. Then I dusted my hands on my jeans. Then I set out across the gravel parking lot. I climbed the stone retaining wall and crossed the lawn to the house. After knocking, I waited a long time before June came to the door. Her mouth wasn't smiling but her eyes seemed glad to see me.

"Mr. Whatnot."

"June," I said. There was a tinge of danger in the whole business. It had nothing to do with her age, which was just a technical matter. A number. I wasn't that much older than she was. "I want to—" I said, my voice rusty from disuse.

"Spit it out." June pressed her forehead to the screen. "What do you want?"

I stood there in filthy cutoffs. "Jesus, you're fantastic," I said. I was still wearing my work gloves.

She burst out laughing and shook her head. She wasn't beautiful, really, not in any ordinary sense. She was tall and big-boned with a too-short haircut. But she had large clear eyes, and an odd cherry mole on the side of her neck. Something small that anyone else might overlook. I wanted to draw her. Not only that, I wanted to paint her. To break out some of those expensive oils I'd been saving up. Cadmium Red, Titanium White.

"Can I come in?"

"I'm sure you *can*," she said, "but you *may* not."

"Thanks for the grammar lesson."

"Where's your friend?"

"My *friend?*"

"Larry."

"What the hell does Larry have to do with anything?" I said. "I don't keep tabs on Larry."

"You don't like Larry, do you?"

"I just don't want to talk about him."

"He's a little weird, isn't he?"

I climbed the bottom step then bent my knee. "*May* I come in?"

She stood barefoot on the cracked linoleum of the kitchen, still in her bathing suit, a thin gold chain around her ankle that I hadn't noticed before. How could I have missed it? It made me want to enter the house all the more. "My mother should be home in a minute."

"Then meet me tonight." I pointed at the barn. "There. At 1:00 a.m."

She doubled over, her hand to her face, laughing so hard that I almost started laughing myself. That's how she closed the inner door, in a gust of laugher.

Turning every so often so as not to break my neck, I walked backward to the barn as June watched from the window.

The rest of the afternoon I spent on the cherry picker, moving from peach tree to peach tree, my least favorite job. The fine fur of the peaches rubbed off and settled into the moist crooks of my arms, which burned and itched with the heat. This part of the orchard afforded no view. With each bundle of small hard peaches I pinched, I thought of June, that gold chain against her smooth white ankle.

Around 6:30, I lowered the bucket of the picker and steered the machine back to the barn, its bulking black wheels chewing the terrain below me. I washed off with the hose, scraping the peach fuzz from my forearms with what fingernails I had. The cool well water felt like a measure of paradise as it rippled along my neck and back. I drank from the nozzle.

"You think I don't know what you're up to?" Larry was sitting on a blue bench seat that had been ripped long ago from a wrecked Thunderbird. "Better stick to peeping."

I turned off the spigot.

"Leave her be," he said.

"Tell me something." I pulled on my t-shirt. "Who died and left you boss?"

Laughing silently, he pointed his finger at me like a gun.

"You're not hearing what I'm saying. You don't listen."

"Don't I?" I was trying to match his thin smile, trying to cover the sadness that had thrust up inside me. He'd taught me everything I knew, about the orchard. "What's it to you?" I said.

"I don't want you wasting the owner's time like that."

I laughed, dry, mirthless, then walked to my bike, mounted it, and pedaled away. I allowed myself one last glance from the road. He hadn't moved.

* * *

That night I set my alarm for 12:30. When it sounded, I rose and showered in the darkness of my apartment. Fifteen minutes later, I was rolling past Larry's Airstream. He would sometimes read all night; on my trips to sketch the fawn's slow decomposition, I'd see his bent head framed by the small windows of the camper, like squares of gold or butter against the black of the orchard. Tonight the Airstream was dark. I got off my ten-speed a hundred yards from the owner's house and wheeled it into the driveway, where I removed my sneakers and shouldered the bike and silently crossed the gravel in my bare feet.

The orchard was quiet, the night without a moon. The humidity of the day dripped in a kind of black coolness from the leaves whenever the wind stirred. No lights in the owner's house. I stood looking for a moment, trying to imagine it long abandoned and collapsing into itself. On the far side of the barn, I dropped the bike and sat in the grass to wait. I told myself whatever happened was fine with me. Five minutes passed, then fifteen. I listened to the hollow scrape of jet engines six miles overhead. The green dial of my watched still glowed faintly—1:21. I got to my feet, my knees aching, and walked to where I could watch the screen door of the house and listen. Nothing. I moved a short distance to the stone retaining wall that ran the length of the yard. There Lillian had planted a line of chrysanthemums that seemed to shimmer, ghostly spheres dissolving and reappearing. Since she'd put the house on the market as a separate property, couples, the women often pregnant, would pull into the driveway to stand with their hands on their hips, exchanging looks before climbing back into their cars and driving away. No one had been inside. Some just slowed and moved on. Lillian and June were flying back to Florida before Labor Day, whether the house, or the orchard, had sold.

Now I saw June drifting toward me across the lawn. Like the chrysanthemums, her skin seemed to glow, her hands and face trailing a faint residue of green light.

"Hey," I whispered, afraid for a moment that she wasn't real.

"Hey." We stood about four feet from each other. She was shivering. "Where should we go?"

I took her hand, and we started out through the middle orchard, down Main Street, as it had been called once. I was shaking now too, which was embarrassing. I walked ahead pulling her gently along as though clearing a path.

"I don't even know you," June whispered.

"I don't know you either." I had in mind a corner of the orchard that cut slightly into the woods to form a brief peninsula of short grass, where I knew we couldn't be easily seen. But the closer we got, the more I began to feel there was something almost incestuous about bringing her there.

"I forgot to tell you," she said. "Larry came by the house tonight."

I stopped. "What?"

"Yeah, he told my mother you've been hitting on me."

"*Hitting on you?*"

"He said she might want to know some things. But he was drunk. He *seemed* drunk. So I'm not sure if my mother really listened. When he finally left, she gave me this look like *what was that* all about? I don't think she took it seriously."

"*Some things?*" I asked. "Like what?"

"I didn't know you'd been arrested."

"Jesus Christ."

"He said you stole equipment."

I was stinging now, my eyes burning.

"Because she owned the orchard now and all that, and she should know, he said." I could barely see June's face, but I knew she was smiling. "Like, hinting that she should find someone else to finish out the season."

"I get the picture," I said.

"I told her later we were just talking. You and me. I said you were too old for me anyway." She pulled me closer. Her jacket hung open, and when I slipped my arms in around her I could feel the heat of her ribs and the disembodied pressure of her breasts against me. At college, I'd had a brief series of dates—if one could even call them that—with a Chinese exchange student from the dorm next to mine, but in all it had lasted less than a month, just a series of sterile flirtations. Once when my roommate was away for the weekend, we spread a blanket on the floor of my dorm room and watched election coverage on a cheap black-and-white TV, and then rolled around for some time while the returns trickled in, running our hands over each other.

June and I lowered ourselves to our knees in the grass. I lay back and she climbed on top of me. I didn't mind that I could barely breathe. We were kissing now. Her taste was complicated, of lip gloss and cigarette smoke, and a staleness that shouldn't have been there.

We heard the sound, at the same time, clearly, and we lay rigid, listening for more.

"What's that?"

I was thinking coyote, but I didn't say anything. I'd never heard one before. We heard it again, this time closer. Or was it a silly, drunken imitation of a coyote?

"All right," I said, rolling from beneath her. "This is ridiculous." The thought of Larry out there watching us was more than I could take.

"No," she said. "Be quiet." She was still on the ground, kneeling, her blouse undone, her bare stomach and hip bones faintly smooth and white. "Don't leave me alone."

At the hem of the orchard, where the rough grass and high weeds ended and the woods began, I pulled the trigger of the flashlight. A yellowy bloom illuminated a skein of brambles and dead cuttings, the trunks of white birches and spruce festooned with vines. The coyote sound stopped. "Follow me."

"Are you for real?"

"OK. Then I'll be right back."

She stood. "No, I think I'll come with you."

"The woods are lovely, dark and deep," I said.

"They're not that lovely."

"You don't know Frost?"

"I'm from Florida. Remember?"

I led her in among the trees, scanning the darkness with the cone of light. "Look," I said, then regretted it immediately. Something large, like something in a bag, hung from a low branch. I wanted to direct the light away from it, but I couldn't. I couldn't look away. There Larry hung by the neck from a length of binding cord, his bare white feet dripping dew into the undergrowth. I stepped closer. Something had come out of the woods to keep him company, and ended up gnawing at his heels and ankles. His blood-fattened face looked over our heads, and the whites of his eyes bulged, sightless as golf balls.

June drew a breath to scream, then another. Again and again I thought she'd let loose into all that blackness, but nothing came out. She could run away if she wanted. I wanted her to run away. I wanted her to leave me there with him. Just me and Larry, as always. The cord chafed and creaked as it twisted. Though he seemed to turn slowly from me, I could not stop staring. His hands hung straight down at his sides, the ring on his stump of a finger catching the light, his shaved head glistening with dew. What I was waiting for, I didn't know. But I felt as ready for it as I'd ever been—as I'd ever be again.

KEEPERS

I

I come out of the Airbnb and turn in a direction I believe to be north. It's Kiev. The broken sidewalk rises with the street. It ramps up and up, then becomes a set of stairs, its warped railing worn smooth under the palms of decades—and, now, under my palms too. My camera bumps my hip. I turn left, I turn right, left, feel the tangible joy of whim. And I wander. The air is cool, fresh, scrubbed, and lemony, but there's a taint of something metallic. There's inscrutable English graffiti. *Lost since 1992.* There are Soviet-era facades with smudged windows that hint at a familiar human chaos inside. On the sills I see plastic bags printed in Cyrillic and empty wine bottles. The older, classical buildings rise arched and filigreed with wrought iron and lovely decay. And on every block, something a little worrying: but maybe it's just me: maybe I'm imagining the men with close-shaven heads who watch my moves from under heavy brows, cellphones pressed to their faces. So smug. Then an inner voice counsels skepticism: no one's looking at you. Know thyself, fool. Walk on.

And I do, I walk, through cool alleyways of concrete and granite. Up camera, down camera. I whisper to myself: That's nice. Look there. Oh, wow. See a pic, take a pic. This is me loosening up.

II

Enter the ravens.

Whose call I seem to have heard already, in my dreams, though I haven't slept yet in Kiev. I've only just arrived. What time is it? No clue. Before me: open-air cage, back alley. I see black feathers like deep indigo. Blue-black. The sudden cock of the head. Black eyes rendering stark appraisal. And that beak. Whoa. It's like a visitation, the real deal, and a serious inconvenience. I'm not sure why, but the word lingers.

There's only one raven. You can feed it cheese—or offer it cheese, anyway. No guarantee the bird will eat it. What do I have? From some inside pocket—wait, seriously?—I produce cheddar, sharp cheddar, wrapped in wax paper, like some character out of Kafka, and up goes the cheddar, to the chicken wire, to the raven wire. My gift. The widow's mite but, like, with dairy. The raven looks away. Oh? Ravens prefer gruyère, do they? Now I'm angry. I have time for this? I turn away, then back.

Screw you! I have tickets to the opera!

Away! Past the raven mural, beneath its towering blues and shapes—and I'm out. In the streets again, hands in my pockets, head down, cobbles underfoot. The light strained and weak. Wood smoke on the air. This way and that. Mindful. Fully awake. But: forward and back—those dudes again with the close-cropped hair, on burner cellphones. A restlessness ripples out.

And then I'm lost. Wonderfully lost. To hell with the Kremlin spies—and everything they represent out in eastern Ukraine. Follow me, will you? Get a life, guys. There's nothing here. My inner fear: they already know that. They're moving on. Wait. You sure?

Along another rise, I sit on a high wall of rough-under-ass concrete, steps away from stairs up into a garden of bamboo. The breeze slurring the leaves behind me.

III

That's when I hear it. Or him, or her. For the first time. A baby's wail. Or *is* it a wail? Maybe it's just a whine.

On my feet again, honing in. I nudge aside the waxy leaves of a fake banana tree. I think it's fake. But not the wail—no, though maybe: it's a little too perfect. Like a cliché, if sounds can be clichés. The city disappears above the foliage. I'm in the middle of one of those "well-kept secrets," a forest within a city, within a forest within a city, etc. And am I liking it? Yes. Four and half stars' worth. I'm all about the acoustics. How the insulation of the biomass amplifies the sound of the baby—or the *recording* of a baby. Evolutionarily high-pitched and eminently identifiable above the woofer tones of surf and turf and city.

No. It's a baby. Swaddled in filthy—what? Swaddles? Swaddling? I kneel, careful, and part the swaddling (it's just cloth, for Christ's sake), and its little baby face emerges. It turns to me, like, what?! Real—or the most fascinating simulation ever. Cyber baby. But rat-faced. An old-man baby. Not cute at all. Par for the baby course; I've been there. I look around. Then this: I think I'm responsible now. No matter who's running the simulation, there's something I have to do. Like what? Something. To make it to the next level. First, pick up the baby. Just lift him up. (Him? Yeah.) Feel the weight of this "tiny person." Cast your mind back to the birth of the baby Nicholas, your only begotten son. The blood and the gore and the shock and the shame—heaping helpings of all that—as I, having entered irrevocably and unprepared that storied, ancient zone, I foundered and I wept.

Not this time. No way. I got this!

You can cradle the baby. *I* can cradle the baby! So clichéd! Does it know English? The baby? Why would it? Because I do! Over the shoulder he goes. You're in it now, bub. I look left and right. Hush, now. Honey chile.

Out on the cobbles again. The freshly tainted air. Heavy metals in the air. The hiss and clop, the horns, the Russian shouts. I follow the tributaries of sound out of the alleyways. They all run downhill into the main streets, into the open, where my rank accountability punks and bloats, more real with each step, the baby comforted, though. Pink and happy, though. For now. And I'm happy—but then I'm suddenly angry. What the hell! Like I have time to babysit? I have people to meet. I have an opera to suffer through!

Oh, so it's all about you, is it?

Where's a Kremlin goon when you need him? They all ran off to headquarters to post reports to Putin. Screw Putin. This way and that, I look—nothing. I gaze. I peer. Even the German tourists in fanny packs don't see me. I tilt the baby forward from my shoulder, part the filthy swaddling again. This kid's performing classic "newborn." Its pink little face, its eyes—they open up on me. OK, I say, what is it that you want? What exactly do you require?

But it's ridiculous. I already know what *he want*. *He want* pabulum. But what is pabulum? It's, like, formula, right? But it's pasty. Yes. It's sweet too—and loaded with processed sugar, but maybe not here. Maybe here it's just chewed food?

Stop. Dial it down. Bring it back. Bring what back? The baby.

Back, yes! Im'a put it *back* in the garden. Are you nuts? No, because please think of the mother. The mother—the mother?—is already, must be, wailing herself. *My child! My child!* In Russian or official Ukrainian. Like a clip from Eisenstein, Odessa Steps sequence. Kind of.

IV

So I do turn back. But good luck with that. Because I'm lost. Up to the corner, turn three times in a circle. Still lost. Wait. You know what? The church! Doorstep, foundling, raised by wolves. The church. Yeah, like in a nineteenth-century novel. Monks. Nuns. Mother Superior's glaring eye (what! another mouth to feed?)—even for just a minute, I can't stand her gaze. No, you will bear it, you will suffer it, then freedom! Cognac at the opera!

Just follow the steeples. That's what they're for—it's like a revelation—the gold onion domes, bulbous, some of them blue, the gold crosses. Look up, look up. The baby on my shoulder again, over my camera strap. Snuggled down. (How you *hated* that word!) I want to take a pic because I see so many pics to take. But I just cross traffic instead—the brand-new Ladas and inscrutable Peugeots. The traffic parts, suddenly aware, all eyes on me now. What's that? Hear that? The raven's—or ravens'—call(s). Oh, now they're calling? Now they're hungry? Screw them and their fussy cheese preferences. Should have taken the cheddar, bitches. I'm on a mission.

Up the curb, among, briefly, people dressed as incomprehensible cartoon characters—are they squirrels? Worn bears? Enough! To the gates of the kingdom. Must one buy a ticket?

To church? Fair enough. For one or for two? For one. Babies enter free. I pass through the turnstile, the old guard all grins and cooing. I move the baby clear of his touch. Out into the air of day again, the inner courtyard, damper, thunderheads framing the inner onion dome of what, whom? Some saint. Saint someone. Sofia?

Inside the church, doesn't matter. The hush of centuries. Motes and dead mold and the cold of the tomb. I'm loving it. Sort of. Because: no photographs. Zero tolerance. The old women stare. The enforcers. It's the same old woman, in multiple iterations, the same blue-gray smock. Rude as Kremlin spies. Can't you see what I have here? I approach one of them. She whisks at bare stone with her pathetic three-straw broom, if that's what you want to call it. See here? I hold up the baby. See? Yes, she sees. They all see. What do you want them to do? Think you can flick a switch and they're at your disposal? Come rushing in to proffer maternal assurances? You think your baby's the only baby that ever lived?

Right now he is! Yeah!

See? one of the replicant women calls. Photo. Here only. She points to a wall of fresh paint—nothing. Blank. It's a joke.

Yeah, but—

Finally, she approaches. She opens her arms. Yes! (Opera! Red velvet! Cognac!) She's not old. She's not young. She's bent over, with that pathetic whisk—are they designed to make *more* work?—hanging from her belt now.

I take.

You take?

I take.

Wait. I don't even know this woman. Are you nuts? Not *my* baby.

I glance up at the Blessed Virgin Mary, resplendent in flecks of actual gold. Nothing but the best for the BVM. So. As I recall: Didn't *she* give *Him* up? Oh, snap. She did, didn't she! Wasn't that the whole point? Thy will be done, and all that?

Here.

And I bridge the gap between us, me and the sweeper woman, the baby between us. Closer now, I can see the confusion in her "timeless" blue eyes. Then, shit, are you kidding me, I miss the baby smell already—the freshness!—as she spirits the child into a fall of rose-colored light. Up goes the camera. It's too good. I'm sorry. Deal with it, Mother Ukraine.

Nyet! another woman yells.

I don't even turn. Busted. I get it. Down goes the camera.

Then something urges my gaze even further upward. Could it be an old woman—yet another old woman—pointing upward? Up past that Virgin Mary there? That one? Up. Yes. I look up— but slowly, I'm taking my own damn time—into the big dome. All right. I'm getting it now, it's beginning to sink in: you're indicating I should look up. Simple enough. To see what, though? Oh. The curve of Christ's face. Oh, and those huge eyes? Got it. This is me, looking up. Hmm. Okay. Seriously? That stillness—I mean, WTF? All right, so you have my attention, "Lord." I go for the camera, but, no, between the motion and the act, the shadow falls. Look. Just look. With your eyes. At all the soot-creased gold enameling. The labor they put into the mosaics. The years. All that. Their lunchbreaks harder than you ever worked.

So can you look away?

Can I—look away? Can I get back to you on that?

The baby starts to wail again, and this time—amplified by the dusty walls and the dome and the gold flake and the roil of motes in shafts of lilac light—it's, well, louder for one. And funny, sort of, and terrifying. And joyful. And it burns, it fucking burns.

But do I look down? Do I avert my eyes? From His eyes? *Can* I look away?

V

It's a simple question.

STRANGE MERCIES

It's terrible the way that prayer is answered.
—Graham Greene, *The Heart of the Matter*

The more Mayhew pretended to pray, the more he doubted the project of *documentation,* and yet the spectacle of what he'd already videotaped seemed fully real only now, the images wavering with unstable pixilation in the low light of his rented room. In one clip, the blood runs in streaks that snake from triangular wounds at the woman's palms *upward* along her wrists and forearms, as though she has held her hands slightly raised and out to the sides long enough for it to dry. Mayhew's neck ached as he sucked the last lozenge of ice from his rum and coke and wiped his forehead with a paper napkin from breakfast. It was night again. He'd lost track of the time. There was no time. He slowed the progression of images to a crawl so he could nudge up to a clear shot of the dark ragged punctures. The woman is eighteen or so, more girl than woman, beautiful to Mayhew in the way all young people were, even more so. She's thin, almost spindly, but with rich folds in her neck that glisten dark gold and deepen when she turns her head to scan the crowd, or looks up into the sky, or meets the gaze of the camera. Even now, it was hard for Mayhew to look at her eyes.

In another clip, rain pocks the buckled concrete just as she's concluding another of her unintelligible what—sermons, he guessed? He had so little Spanish. For five minutes, she had watched Mayhew with squinting suspicion and maybe a little superiority and certainly a degree of pity as he crouched in the street, duck-walked closer, angled to the left or right, dipped low, then held the camera above the heads of the onlookers. At the time, he wasn't paying full attention to the content of the shot, just that it was well framed and in focus, the sweat streaming from his temples into his beard, then leaking from his chin.

Now she stands on a splintered wooden spool tipped on its side.

Now she's talking to the crowd of mostly old women, some apparently blind, their eyes wandering, and to legless men in grimed soccer jerseys on the curb, their skin like jerky, the tattered hems of their pants folded back under their knees, and to ambulatory cripples, street people resting puckered stumps on the cross-bars of their crutches.

Now a woman in her eighties turns half-smiling to the camera and lifts her dress to reveal the archipelago of running sores that traces the ridgeline of her shins. In that moment, weeks before, Mayhew hadn't had time to take it all in. It was almost too painful to watch, like some medieval pageant of horrors, but he watched again and again, for hours. Mostly, though, he watched because she is fascinating. The alarming nonchalance of her gesticulation is fascinating. She's in control, but more than this. She radiates. In her Jordache jeans and home-sewn *camiseta*, the white ear bud wires of an iPhone draped over her shoulder—she seems outside time looking in. This is serenity. The more he looked, the more radiant she became. He found it difficult to put a label to what he felt—other than shame, because he wondered whether such thinking might be the ghost of colonialism talking shit in his head.

He'd shot the woman over a number of days, while the network correspondent, Bob Yoshida, whose Spanish was also practically nonexistent, shouted questions and the locals all around them curled their lips in disgust. She was not someone who granted interviews. In one—only one—clip does fresh blood well up from the wounds unmistakably and in real time, twenty-one seconds worth; it drips to the street with each gesture of her arms—some of it splattering people as they beam into this chance benediction. (Washed in the blood, he'd thought, with a wince. There'd been dried blood that night on the barrel of Mayhew's lens.) Now she's shifting painfully from one foot to the other, two red-brown stains where the blood has surfaced through the bandages.

But not long after Mayhew shot the footage, she had disappeared. It all seemed to happen at once, a rushing confluence of events. There was an email from the network calling him and Yoshida back to Chicago, which Mayhew had refused to obey. Soon the network's emails stopped, and in the weeks since, he had not left the walled city's square mile, its morning smells of shoe polish and fresh-squeezed lime. He was a little unclear about the terms of his visa. He convinced himself not to worry. He was talented that way. He would find her. She was here, somewhere. He needed more footage. He thought he had time enough and, with one exception, everything he needed in his small room on one of the narrower streets near the cathedral. The air conditioning was weak and intermittent, but Bob had left behind two and a half cases of bottled water. The man had been scrupulous about not drinking from the tap. "Hydrate!" he would yell whenever he saw Mayhew break a sweat. Then his voice softened into ironic fecklessness: "But don't drink the water." Considering it a cliché, Mayhew had not heeded that warning. He'd rinsed his toothbrush at the sink, and spent a week and a half navigating, like a cripple himself, a new universe of bacterial consequences. "Baptism by fire," he'd yelled from the toilet. There was also the beer, Aguila, not great but entirely serviceable. And, of course, Mayhew's supply of rum, the good stuff, Ron Medellín. He and Bob had split the cost of a case, even though Bob himself, knightly Bob, rarely drank. (It had taken Mayhew all of one day, but he'd learned to operate the goddamn twist cap—at about the same time he'd determined that *Ron* wasn't Señor Medellín's Christian name.) For entertainment, aside from the editing and re-editing that occupied most of his time, he'd brute-forced access into a Wi-Fi network from one of the surrounding hotels. The connection almost always worked, and no one seemed to be monitoring the bandwidth he regularly chewed up. Now that Bob was gone, Mayhew gorged himself on all the amateur porn he could consume, usually late nights, or sometimes right after morning mass at San Pedro Claver, his horniest time of the day, when he'd seek refuge from the day's heat and ubiquitous light like some inarticulate cave animal. The heat was something he'd not grown accustomed to. He was used to Chicago summers, the legions of elderly fading away in their narrow hovels. But this was something entirely other, an all-out frontal, almost ontological, assault on corporeality, a late-morning movie trailer for the Last Judgment. It was fucking hot.

★ ★ ★

Mayhew convinced himself he missed nothing of his former life—the hour commute, the notional cheese and tasteless supermarket tomatoes, the scrape and blare of the El, talk radio. Almost nothing. After the producer's emails stopped, some part of him knew the video would never see the light of day. But he was beyond concern—he told himself this—and he felt that only now could he get down to the real work. International Catholic Broadcast Network? ICBN? God bless them, but the swill they served up 24/7 staggered the mind. (He never watched it himself.) One of the producers had spoken of the network as "the Fox News of American Catholic broadcasting." This was assumed to be a point of pride. Their audience "for now," the suit explained, was, in a phrase Mayhew particularly admired, the "low-information consumer of religious media." And while they were idiots, they were all God's children, with not insignificant disposable incomes. So, the reasoning went, Mayhew could lose his elitist pretentions in a hurry. And who the hell was *he*, anyway?

During the job interview the year before, the network hadn't seemed to give a shit if he attended mass. Or even if he was Catholic. He was—Roman Catholic—though any such self-identification arose more from a vague and residual feeling of clannish nostalgia than from actual conviction. He was just a guy, like any other guy. In a conference room looking out across the beige steel of the Loop, the gray of Lake Michigan beyond, he'd sat across from the ICBN HR person, a perpetually kinetic woman with ironic eyes and acid tone, and a hell of a tailor—this turned out to be Jasmine, in her finest raiment. Also present: the executive producer, a man about Mayhew's age, name of Timothy, Mr. Timothy, who looked like could bench three hundred pounds in his button-down oxford without breaking a sweat. What the hell had Mayhew expected? Nuns with clipboards? Tonsured monks in bulky headphones? The network had advertised for a cameraman. Here he was in a new tie. He'd been laid off from his job providing AV support at Columbia College, basically setting up digital projectors for professorial Power-Point presentations and reformatting user-hosed hard drives. It had been months since he'd known the joys of biweekly direct deposit. He would have told Jasmine whatever she wanted to hear. He took it as evidence of divine intervention that no one checked his references—a fortunate development in that these were fictional characters. How hard could it be to hold the camera steady?

In that meeting, Jasmine had spoken at length from boiler-plate she'd internalized the way people once knew the Apostles' Creed. Mindshare, *soulshare,* eyeballs, deliverables. Product. He'd felt a little woozy. Did he know that ICBN had recently launched—"set loose" were Jasmine's words—its own version of EWTN's Mother Angelica, though with a somewhat harder-core on-air presence? In five years, Jasmine crowed, no one would know or care who came first. Sister Payne. *Can she bring it!* He'd caught glimpses of the woman's pasty countenance glowering from the ceiling-corner flat screens, news ticker tracking every jot and titter of the pontiff's Asian visit. The second week on the job, he'd even passed the sister herself in the halls on one of her rare visits to flyover country, caffeinated entourage trailing behind with their cradled tablet PCs. Not a simulation, mind you, this was an actual nun. They'd only recently moved her show to an afternoon slot. The format was straightforward: she opened with a decade of the rosary, then fielded rambling call-in questions from whiners about the rhythm method and mas-turbation. The same shtick every day. She'd come off all quiet and understanding at first, but then, carefully folding her bony fingers, smiling Sister Payne tore them all a new one. Mayhew immediately understood the appeal; he recognized in it some-thing deeply satisfying. The first time he heard them queue the bridge from "Breakout" by Swing Out Sister as segue to a commercial, he thought he'd wet his business casuals.

★ ★ ★

A week or so after Bob's departure, Mayhew's HD camera had been stolen out of his room. Now he carried its much smaller replacement with him on his twice-daily peregrinations through the city. When the heat wasn't insufferable, after morning mass and the retinal shock of reentry into the glare of the Caribbean daylight, he'd walk the walls, unthinking. He favored the wide west-facing battlements, the horizon like a vision worked over with Photoshop's smudge tool. He learned to hug the shadowed side of the street, noted the migration of juice vendors over the course of the day, heliotropes bending to the will of the sun. One of his favorite stops was the Palace of the Inquisition, where he marveled at the many tools of torture, the mysterious tongs and spiked collars, the cells of mercy and of penitence.

At night, among the tangle of café chairs and tables that appeared at dusk in the shelter of the same walls and disappeared long before sunrise, he drank Cuba libres for which he was ceremoniously overcharged. It seemed in keeping with his duties as clueless American exile. The waiters loved to see him arrive, with their smiles and obscene gestures beyond his periphery. He'd gotten chummy with a shockingly thin man from Medellín who shined shoes for tourists and with whom he carried on brief, awkward conversations and, later, hours-long games of chess, which, even after he'd begun to try to win, Mayhew always lost. That he'd already grown used to the routine and anonymity of these days worried him. From the beginning, his cellphone had been useless. Soon his wife's emails stopped altogether.

He replaced the stolen camera with a pro-am model of lesser

quality that he bought from one of the young street vendors. Where the kid had gotten it, Mayhew neither knew nor cared. *"¿Que quiere?"* the kid had said. It was nearly midnight. He'd been tailing Mayhew for two blocks, a youth of about thirteen, two years older than Mayhew's own son.

"Nada," said Mayhew, and went all brittle. He'd had it with the vendors approaching him. One, then another, then another. In waves. He'd bought his share of coconut shell rosaries and faux pastel street scenes and three-CD sets of the local vallenato talent. As word spread that he was no longer an easy mark, the waves had lessened. Yet he wanted them to know he wasn't like the other Americans they'd met. For some reason it seemed important to prove this to these strangers.

The kid wore a fitted University of Texas baseball cap, its flattened bill turned slightly sideways. *"Dígame,"* he said, keeping pace with Mayhew. *"¿Que quiere?"* Soon there was a man walking on the other side as well. He wore a bandana around his leathery neck and seemed spry for his age, which was advanced, and his eyes shone under each passing streetlamp. He had the face of someone with too much control of his own expression, someone overconfident in his skill at hiding behind it.

"You want girls?" he said.

Mayhew immediately despised the man's smile. Everything about him spoke of the kind of conspiratorial male carnality that had always embarrassed Mayhew. Though even in this, he was of two minds. Here, over the weeks, he'd come to admire the language of street glances and the ostentatious—almost ceremonial—display of male appreciation for all the many women one saw during the course of a public day. The sheer variety and wonder of it. He'd convinced himself he'd joined the ranks of these South American men, however provisionally, these Caribbean men who unlike their U.S. counterparts dressed like adults. He'd bought a few guayaberas himself; they seemed to bestow upon his squirrelly personality something of the same mystique of masculine pride and maturity. But he knew it was a sham.

Now the kid and the man competed for Mayhew's attention, seemingly oblivious of one another.

"What do you want?" the kid asked again, trying out his English.

The man touched Mayhew's arm. "No hoes, *señor*. University girls." Man to man, he seemed to be saying: we all want the same thing.

"University girls?" Mayhew rolled his eyes. "Right." But if he were honest with himself—and maybe that was what he admired about the men down here, their honesty—the company of an attractive woman just then did not seem entirely unappealing. He wasn't honest with himself, though, he'd never been, and he knew he'd suffer for it someday. He'd not cheated on his wife in all the years of their marriage. At this remove, though, he'd taken up the daily refreshment and the small consolation as never before—of admiring the asses of passing women, the beautiful Latinas. Not to do so would have been rude.

The kid giggled, frustrated but keeping pace. He'd seen Mayhew's type before. American chump supreme. He tried another angle: "What do you *need?*" he asked. He seemed to be on the verge of giving up.

"University girls," said the man. "Guaranteed. No hoes."

"That's kind of you, but no," Mayhew said. He tried out some of the high school Spanish he'd been itching to use. He'd made a pact with himself never to pretend to know the language, but he broke it again and again. "*Tengo esposas.*"

"*¡Muy paila!*" The kid laughed out loud. He yelled something to a circle of hang-dog men sitting in flimsy lawn chairs at the corner of a side street, who laughed in unison. Then back to Mayhew: "*¿Cuántos tiene?*"

"I have everything I need."

The man keeping pace on Mayhew's left tried not to smile. "It must be nice."

"*Claro,*" said the kid, "but what do you *want?*"

Mayhew stopped short to look squarely at the kid, who seemed to shy away under the sudden attention. "A digital movie camera," he said. "A video camera."

The kid's eyes lit up. He smiled and ran off into the night, the soles of his sneakers flashing.

The next morning, coming out of mass at the cathedral, Mayhew observed the same boy approaching from afar, a shiny white and blue box balanced on his head. "You're shitting me," he said. "You are too much."

"No, *mijo.* Do you remember last night?" The kid swung the box down and held it out proudly. "Digital camera. Video camera."

It wasn't close to what Mayhew usually shot with—the work-horse Panasonic HPX300—but it would do. It was certainly a lot lighter. And whatever down-market drift in picture quality it represented might lend an air of textured amateur authenticity to whatever he shot next. "*¿Cuánto cuesta?*" he asked.

"How much do you *want* to pay?"

"How much do I want to pay? I don't *want* to pay anything. Let's skip the games. You tell me."

"No, you tell me how much do you want to pay." The kid fought with his growing impatience. The American was an ass-hole, but he had money. An old story.

Mayhew knew what the kid would do before he said it: "30,000."

The boy looked insulted. He shook his head. Mayhew had to admit, the kid was good.

In the end, Mayhew counted out $100 American in twenties. He slipped the camera out of the box and shot a few seconds of the kid dancing with ironic intensity until what little power was left in the battery failed, and the kid jogged off with the five twenties clamped in his fist, laughing over his shoulder. Mayhew was happy with the deal he'd made. Everybody was happy.

Later, when Mayhew's medication ran out, the kid proved to be just as helpful. One afternoon Mayhew showed him the pills in question, wrote the name down in block letters, and the kid brought back the same purple discs, same size, same weight. Mayhew had even taken them for a while, but when he ran out again, he told himself he was done with all that. The daily encounter with the heat had cleared his head, burned away the dross. And soon the anxiety he'd known until seven or eight years before began to creep back; a dread as physical as heartburn, it hunkered in the black vacuum above his abdomen, justifying every abortive attempt at descriptive synesthesia. He'd been a sad piece of shit indeed. Now he was back in true form.

When his wife's emails stopped, it was a different matter. He'd known he could push her without serious repercussions— she loved him, he knew this, too—but he'd not known how far. It had been an out-of-body experiment to plumb the limits of her patience, to finger the festering wound. The last time they'd spoken, he'd called her from an old payphone at the bodega three blocks from his apartment and reversed the charges. The same bodega where he and Bob had bought the Medellín rum. He stood staring at a rack of unlabeled bottles and an old man with cottony white eyebrows who sat in the smoke and gloom of a free corner. She picked up on the second ring. He said her name, and she was silent for a moment. Finally, she said, "I don't even know what to say to you."

"I know you don't," he said. "That's clear." The old man's face was as still and stained as a limestone wall. Mayhew didn't know whether to acknowledge him, now that his eyes had fully adjusted to the low light.

"Do you check your fucking email?" She'd never been a woman to cry or curse. She was the person he'd been closest to in his life, but there were times when she became a stranger, sent him away shivering as he shivered now, standing on another continent, wondering what did this say about his "capacity for intimacy"? About him as a human being? *Was* he one? Why was he doing this? "I won't even ask the obvious question."

"Good," he said. The mouthpiece smelled of whiskey. "I wouldn't know how to answer it."

"Well, then that's settled—"

"How are things?"

She laughed—or cried out. He couldn't tell. "Things here are *ridiculous.*"

"How so?" he asked. He knew damn well how so. She was being understanding for a woman in her position. He wanted to hear her being understanding for a few moments more. He was a shit, had always been one, deep down. The one way to make it up to her, to everyone: return bearing miraculous tidings, proof to leave them all speechless. He'd have to come home one of the three fucking kings.

"We're about two weeks away from being foreclosed on, you know," she said. "I've been moving all our shit to a storage unit off the frontage road."

He winced. Compartmentalize, he told himself. "If I had money I'd send it."

"The account is almost empty. The network stopped direct deposit. I tried to get Jasmine on the phone, but she wouldn't even talk to me. Why is that? I'm like this pariah. I just wanted to know how long we're covered, for health insurance. What did you say to them? I hate feeling like that—helpless. I tried calling Bob but—"

"Jesus, don't bother Yoshida," he said. Something about the idea of her on the phone with Bob made him queasy. It spoke of rupture and contamination. "Here's what I have to say: the project isn't finished. OK? It's that simple. I need to complete what I've started. I can't just quit now. I don't work that way. Not anymore. Just don't be calling Bob."

She waited for him to finish. "Are you having an affair with someone down there?"

He snorted. Affairs were for above-average-looking guys who worked out three times a week, wore aftershave lotion, and watched SportsCenter religiously. He didn't have affairs. She knew better, and at that moment he hated her for it.

"Mike's not sleeping," she said. "He's a mess."

At the mention of his son, Mayhew felt an almost unbearable loneliness, as though suddenly aware of the continent's weight, a world devoid of a single person who knew his name. Exactly the feeling he'd been hoping to avoid. That he might weep seemed a clear and present danger. She knew what she was doing. When it became obvious a response from him was not forthcoming, she finally lost it for real, and fell to hissing, spitting. The gnashing of teeth. She dropped the receiver, picked it up without missing a beat. If he were dead, things would be a lot easier, a childish thought, he knew, but a familiar one. This might be all part of the process of his removal from the world of light.

"I shouldn't have to explain," he said. "Don't you believe in miracles? You're Catholic."

If she'd begun to calm down, this set her off afresh. "You *fucking* asshole," she said. "The woman was doing it *to herself.* What part of that don't you get? She was carving holes in her palms with whatever—a fucking steak knife." Jasmine had posted a brief blog entry to this end, and the word had gone forth. The network never mentioned it again. Reuters and the other wires seemed pleased to let it go. The Vatican investigators had been called back to Rome—if they'd ever left. (Mayhew imagined a priest in a beige raincoat eating a first-class dinner on an evening transatlantic Alitalia flight.) His wife wasn't exactly the most devout woman he'd ever met; still, he decided not to tell her how after mass he'd speedwalk back to the apartment with the unchewed host. He barely thought of it himself. This was between himself and the Lord, who might or might not exist. He hadn't been to confession in years, so in a sense he *was* obeying the doctrinal prohibition against receiving communion with mortal sin on one's soul. If by *receiving* they meant digesting. He took it on his tongue, he just didn't swallow. In a clear Tupperware container on top of the room's only closet, he kept a growing collection of moist hosts.

"Calm down," he said. "That's enough." But she took no heed and he had no choice but to speak into her ravings. "I have the fucking footage. I can sit and watch it happen. I do every night. The wounds open by themselves. There's no knife. It's clear for all to see." But to touch the mystery this way—with such words—seemed to him unclean. It wasn't the whole truth. "It *will* be," he said.

"Fantastic! Come share it with us, hon."

"I need more," he said. "I'm not finished."

There came a commotion on the other end, his son's voice, and a muffled grappling for the phone. "Wait. Mike wants to talk with you."

"No," Mayhew said. "Tell him I'm sorry. I have to go." He hung up. He took five steps toward the door, jerked to a stop as though reaching the end of a tether, walked back to the phone and picked up. Nothing. No dial tone. "Hello?" The old man in the corner hadn't changed expression. He continued to stare straight ahead; his eyebrows hung like flattened balls of tobacco-stained cotton, as if Mark Twain were South American, and not dead. The man might have been dead himself. "Hello, Mike?" His face wet with perspiration, Mayhew hung up again and walked out into a street whose gutters ran with foul-smelling water and bits of lettuce. There were lights on strings that spanned the square, and a mouthy group of European tourists—big-boned Scandinavians in bright hiking apparel— were drinking themselves blind. One of the taller men was forcing himself to walk an imaginary tightrope with the encouragement of a young café hostess. And a little black dog lay on its side, as still as a carcass. The tourists had commandeered Mayhew's usual table, intruders not only into the sanctity of his café but invaders of his city. He smiled. His city? Why not? To sin in a foreign place lodged something of it in your soul. You could never leave it behind. The more serious the sin, the more inextricable the lodging. When the Scandinavian guy stumbled onto its rat tail, the dog leapt up with a horrifying yip and scrambled away while everyone laughed.

***

The next evening unfolded with the logic of dreams. Mayhew

did not notice her until she'd already passed, the scent of jasmine lingering in her wake as she traced a line of shadow just within the walls of the city, her heels clicking on the cobbles. He'd lingered in the café later than usual, immersed in a complicated game of chess with the shoeshine man from Medellín whom in his mind he called Ruy Lopez—because the man often used an opening attributed to the sixteenth-century Spanish monk of that name. Tonight they'd played their usual silent match, punctuated by moments of awkwardness and grimaces of resignation. They seemed beyond the need to talk. During the game Mayhew had allowed himself to imagine that he might someday find a home here in the walled city, though he knew that in the real world—this one—such a thing was not possible. He didn't belong here. He didn't belong anywhere. He checked Ruy with a rook, glanced over the man's shoulder, and saw her walking away along the edge of the wall's shadow, her elbow locked into the arm of a man obscured by darkness. Her laughter danced above the voices of the café patrons, the ringing of flatware. Mayhew stood up. After a few involuntary steps in her direction, he stopped. What exactly would he say? Briefly he met Ruy's alarmed eyes, then started off without looking back, his video camera slung over his shoulder.

A block and a half farther along the wall, he picked up the scent of her perfume, caught sight of her and the man slipping into one of the pedestrian gates out of the city, which were deep enough to harbor bookstalls and souvenir shops during the day. The man with her was much older. He wore a linen suit in serious need of laundering and mesh loafers. Mayhew paused at the outer gate, the medicinal smell of mold and tropical rot rich and alive. For weeks, his self-confinement within the city walls had been like a vow—to whom he refused to acknowledge. This couldn't be the same woman. Was he out of his mind? This couldn't be the stigmatist. This was a prostitute. But in the instant it took to turn back toward the café, he realized he was wrong; and without another moment's hesitation, he drifted beyond the city's fortification.

It *was* the same woman; there was no doubt. From the video, he knew every nuance of her posture and expression, most of all her eyes, which he'd eventually allowed himself to look into. Hanging thirty yards back, he followed them along a congested street, Vespas and smoking taxis narrowly avoiding the crossfire of pedestrians, to a steeply pitched ramp that climbed the westward wall. Up top, a crowd of tourists watched African dancers in white muslin pivot and thrust as a battery of drums echoed against the houses on the near side and vendors jammed straw hats onto the heads of sweaty onlookers. Mayhew circled the gathering, shaking off his own plague of vendors and angling for a view of the woman's hands, one of which hung now from the man's neck. He watched her draw the man closer, flash her tongue in his ear. The man didn't stop her; he seemed bored as he watched a female dancer gyrate her hips over someone's supine body. Mayhew pressed closer. A cool wind ruffled the edge of the woman's skirt. He wanted to see the scabbed-over flesh. He imagined himself forcing it open again with his tongue. The next time she went up on her toes to whisper in the man's ear, Mayhew stood at arm's length directly behind them. He watched her hand smooth the rumpled linen between the man's shoulder blades. A vendor whispered something in Mayhew's ear, a scrawny man wielding a large bottle of water in each hand: *"El agua."*

"Do you mind?" said Mayhew, pulling away. "Jesus Christ, I'm trying to see something here."

The woman turned. Their glances caught, but then she was already looking past him at another performer, a man eating flames with relish in his shining eyes.

* * *

Through the night and into the morning, he went over the old footage as though for the first time, freezing each frame that only the day before had presented itself as a window into mystery, enlarging it, enhancing it. He drank too much rum. Drunk, he allowed himself to luxuriate in the ambiguities, his whole pathetic life balanced on a knife-edge between childlike faith and sneering mockery, whiplashing from nihilist to penitent in the breath of a single sentence, jeering at the grotesqueries of religious belief—the silly hats, the psychopathic prohibitions against the smallest joys, Amish suspenders, dervish slippers, the fountains of undisguised misogyny, and the threadworn political expediencies of church-and-state history—then regretting the utterance before it had fully left his lungs. Madness. He'd waited long enough for the mustard seed to take root. The world couldn't be moist with the presence of God *and* a desert void and mechanistic—and yet each embrace came with its own repudiation. He'd fingered the sore, worked to death a million reasons why it didn't make a damn bit of difference, but he knew that was bullshit. You could blather on about the power of myth and the reifying nature of language, but in the end, in *this* world, either the wounds in the woman's palms were there or not, self-inflicted or not. Either the author of the universe was watching him right now—or not.

The air conditioning in his room had failed; and without the insulating white noise, he was aware of the call of the curlews—an ethereal sound, almost human. He stepped into the predawn dew, the moon sharp, orange, prehistoric. The city stretched away like a series of empty hallways he was cursed to wander.

★ ★ ★

At mass the next morning, he sulked in the last row of pews, alone. Weekday services were cavernous and poorly attended. He'd drunk too much of the *ron* the night before; the edges of his vision still lagged like aging videotape whenever he turned his head too sharply. He hadn't slept more than half an hour, and after watching with chaste fascination a dozen or so internet clips depicting a practice informally known as pegging (men penetrated anally by women outfitted with crotch-harnessed dildos), he'd been in and out of dreams involving the stigmatist and his wife, who soon morphed into a single person. His dream life had never been narrative or particularly intelligible—and as such always conveniently forgettable, more a series of jump cuts and rough edits—but the overall vibe the night before, even in those few minutes of sleep, had been charged with erotic giddiness of a kind he'd not experienced since his first wet dreams, a sinfulness the texture of healing oils that welled up through unseen apertures or of warm honey laying down a slick layer of sweetness, entirely without guilt or consequences, a balm for his troubled joints, it seemed, and akin to the lost memories of maternal embrace. He'd awakened, ashamed suddenly by his suspicion that the Tupperware container on the top shelf of the closet had all along been emitting a slowly intensifying radium-green glow, the awareness of which had distracted him from an image looming at the similarly green horizon of his dream consciousness, of an unspeakable act involving the woman's wounds.

He'd come to mass late, leaving ajar one of the cathedral's tall wooden doors. The way the sunlight silhouetted his head and shoulders in sharp outline against the back of the pew in front of him stung like judgment, a reckoning that this was all he'd ever be—a passing shadow—and all the destiny he deserved, the hell he'd been building all his life. He lost himself halfway through an Act of Contrition, then switched to the Jesus Prayer; it was shorter. As though talking in his sleep, the priest tumbled along in Spanish, the air thickening. Mayhew did not take communion but spent an hour on his knees before the Blessed Sacrament in the dark of the small chapel, the rays of the monstrance like gold daggers.

Outside, when he emerged, it was nearly noon. Sunlight scoured the square. If he did not move with the certainty of a destination, they'd be on him. But he dawdled, leaning against one of the rust-hued sculptures, a metallic dentist readying a robotic patient for bridgework. As though summoned, seemingly from nowhere, the boy who'd sold him the video camera approached. He looked older, taller. If he recognized Mayhew, he gave no indication.

"*¿Que mas?*" he asked flatly. Then, the age-old question: "*¿Que quiere?*"

Mayhew looked around. Every passerby seemed now to be listening. Cold air spilled like dense milk from the doors to the church, the priest cocking an ear from the sacristy. Even Saint Peter Claver stared down from his alcove beneath the circular stained-glass window. Mayhew smiled ruefully. "Not a goddamn thing."

"No, *mijo*," the boy said. "*Quiere algo. Digame.*"

"Fine. You want to know what I want?" Mayhew spoke quickly, not caring whether the boy understood. "Do you remember the night I asked for a camera?"

The boy squinted. "*Si.*"

"There was another man."

"Si, recuerdo." He seemed suddenly bored. He hadn't antici-
pated carrying on an actual conversation with this creepy Anglo.
But then he smiled. *"Me dijo que tenía 'esposas.'* Then I ask you
how many."

"Yes. That man asked me something else too."

The boy lost his smile. He stared into Mayhew's eyes. "University girls?" he asked weakly.

"Yeah, but—" Mayhew looked around again.

"Ahora?"

"No, no, not now, but I'm looking for one woman in
particular."

The boy wiped his nose and nodded.

"I have a picture of her, a video." Mayhew hadn't planned to
take things in this direction. "Can I show it to you?"

"To me?"

"Yes."

"Ahora?"

"I live around the corner. It's where I'm staying. It won't take
long."

The boy's face had shed the last of its affect.

"Just come up for a minute and look at the picture."

Mayhew led him out of the flat light of the square and along
his narrow street, a journey of three hundred yards, but he kept
having to slow for the boy to catch up. Nothing about it felt
right, but he couldn't stop. They walked beneath the arched
doorway, past two men on their padded knees replacing a broken floor tile in the courtyard, up the iron stairs, which rang as
they climbed to the second floor, and then around the gallery
to Mayhew's room. He unlocked the door and went in; the boy
followed behind leaving it open.

The air reeked of unwashed clothing and spilled rum. The

kid was the first other person to enter the apartment since Bob. Mayhew slid his laptop out from beneath a face-down copy of Unamuno, and opened it up, the monitor glowing as it awoke. "*Siéntese,*" he said. But the boy remained standing, gloomy and hunched, an outline in the doorway. He didn't seem like the same person. Mayhew called up the editing software, located the clip of the woman that had obsessed him, and beckoned it forth. Then he arranged the laptop on the edge of the end table so they could both watch. As the boy squinted, the footage danced in the wetness of his eyes. Mayhew froze the image on a closeup of the woman's face, just before a cutaway to her bleeding hands.

"Do you know her?" Mayhew asked.

"*Pienso tan,*" he said, rolling his index finger. "Show me more."

Mayhew set the video in motion again, and absently the boy began to nod his head. When the footage cut to the woman's hands and the blood dripping into the street, he looked up at Mayhew, his eyes empty.

"I'm a reporter," Mayhew said. "I was sent to do a story on this woman. That's why I needed the camera. She's disappeared, but I think I saw her the other day. Do you know her? Have you seen this woman before?"

The boy bit the corner of his lip. He bobbed his head left, right, as though weighing his limited options. He stood up and moved to the door. There he paused to look back, his face showing all the affect of a corpse. "You come tonight," he said, finally.

Mayhew wanted to ask the boy what was wrong, but all he could say was "It's important."

The boy was already gone.

Mayhew set his travel clock and slept wedged up against the wall until the alarm awoke him. He rose and showered. As he toweled off, the strange insects—part ant, part termite, part aphid—were at it again, traveling in a line from the floor to the ceiling. He hadn't done laundry in weeks. Everything felt damp and grimy. A patina of mold had blossomed on his towel. He dressed in white guayabera and dark jeans. He hadn't eaten, but he wasn't hungry. He poured himself some rum in a tall sticky water glass and swallowed it in a single gulp, his eyes on the Tupperware atop the closet.

The night air smelled of ocean salt and burnt brazil nuts. The streets had begun to fill with tourists—Anglo couples, the guys of indeterminate age in straggly beards, the girls in gauzy wrap-around skirts and flip-flops; the Europeans with their supercilious airs; the locals, men with quick, hungry eyes; the vendors tacking from mark to mark. Citronella torches burned above the outdoor tables and chairs, and pretty young women stood in high heels on the cobbles in front of adjacent cafés with their menus and tight t-shirts and flirting smiles, eager for eye contact with anyone passing by.

He hadn't intended to visit his usual table—there wasn't time—but habit sent him past his café. From across the street, he saw a man who looked like Bob Yoshida sitting with Ruy Lopez, and he veered into one of the gates before either of them caught sight of him. Not just Bob—Jasmine stood behind them with her lovely arms folded. They were speaking to two other men as well with whom Mayhew had a passing acquaintance and whom he believed to be members of the city's plainclothes police force. He lingered in the vaulted space as though stunned by a blow to the forehead, a pressure in his ears, not entirely sure if he was awake or not. None of it made sense. This overlapping of worlds. He watched them interview Ruy, who sat before a chessboard and pieces set in initial position. The man seemed unusually animated tonight, his thin arms and polish-stained hands working the air. Mayhew wondered how long Jasmine and Bob had been in his city. Did they know where he was staying? Had he told Ruy? He activated his camera, raised it to his eye, thumbed the zoomed. But the light was too low. He switched to night vision and thought to read Jasmine's lips. Her face hovered, green-grained and ugly. The next minute he was gone.

The boy sat on the high curb at a corner near the old hospital, on a street that dead-ended into one of the larger battlements along the wall. When he saw Mayhew approaching, he slipped into a metal doorway, and reappeared with an older man whom Mayhew thought he recognized.

"Forgive me for asking," the man said, smiling, his hand out. "What happened to all your wives?" He wore a long, pale-yellow guayabera with dark-orange Chinese characters instead of the vertical pleats. He waved Mayhew along; they started to walk, the boy forgotten already. "Did they leave you? Every one of them? Aren't you lonely now?"

"All good things must come to an end," said Mayhew, looking away. He was trying to contain his visceral distaste for the man. "Did the boy tell you what I'm after?"

"Yes," said the man, nodding thoughtfully. "Yes, he did."

"I don't do this normally. In fact, I've never done this before. I'm not even doing it now."

"You don't have to explain to me." They turned into a narrow street, dark with floral vines draped from wrought-iron balconies. "I like your shirt," the man said. He slipped a short, fat, aromatic cigar from his guayabera pocket and slid it into one of Mayhew's with a pat. "You're a long way from home, my friend."

"He told you who I'm looking for?"

Smiling, the man waved away Mayhew's concern. "There is something for everyone."

"Yeah, well, I'm not here for—"

"It's OK." He slowed to put his arm around Mayhew, who stiffened. "It's OK." Like two old friends, they walked on, Mayhew in the damp gutter; the man, shorter, walking along the high edge of the curb, his arm on Mayhew's neck and Mayhew undecided about how or whether to free himself. There were no tourists along the route they followed. The streets were deserted. Not only were all the doors closed tight; they seemed to have been welded shut long ago. The man said he'd lived in Philadelphia and Miami for a time when he was in his twenties. He asked Mayhew where he was from, but didn't wait for an answer.

"What about this?" the man asked, tapping Mayhew's video camera. "You like to preserve the memory?"

Mayhew handed it over, not knowing why. "I take it everywhere."

"It's up to her." The man examined the camera briefly then handed it back. "She says. Yes or no."

Along the westward wall, they came to the nearly hidden side entrance of a massive yellow house. The sodium lights from the highway beyond illuminated its upper story, where large regions of paint had cracked and flaked away. One of the patches looked like a central Asian nation or autonomous region. Mongolia, Kazakhstan. The man dipped his head and knocked on the double door, then opened it immediately, and they crossed the threshold into a familiar smell of mold and fresh cooking. He stopped with his hand on Mayhew's chest and leaned forward with an almost menacing air, and Mayhew knew to ask him how much. He did. The man told him, his voice less solicitous now. Mayhew didn't argue, though he immediately forgot the amount and pressed a wad of damp American twenties into the man's palm.

They navigated a poorly lit hallway without doors or windows, which opened into a courtyard that they crossed between bougainvillea plants in oversized pots and banana trees whose sickly roots bulged up through the terracotta tiles. Three silent pigeons twisted their heads and beaks to lap at a shallow puddle. Through a yellow half-door, and they were inside again, a room surprisingly dark. The sole source of light came from a small black-and-white television that broadcast a rectangle of noiseless static, the kind of snowy field he remembered waking to in his youth. The man grinned and clicked his tongue. He winked and patted Mayhew on the shoulder, then leaned in again to whisper something Mayhew didn't understand, his breath smelling of tea and cigars. With a disquieting smile, he withdrew, closing the door softly behind him.

For a long time, Mayhew waited as though for a signal. "Hello?" he said, finally. "I'm here." This struck him as idiotic. He slipped the video camera from his shoulder and dangled it over the couch, then thought better of this and slung it again over his shoulder. Through an arch that separated one room from the next, he shuffled forward. There in a shallow parlor sat a young woman at a kitchen table, her bare legs crossed at the knees. She pulled one of the iPhone ear buds from her ear and smiled falsely. She'd been tending to her nails. Mayhew inched closer. An electric surge rose in his chest, blossoming into acid. His ears began to ring. It was she. He was sure of it.

"Hello," he said, bowing ridiculously. On the table three bottles of Aguila beer stood in puddles of their own condensation next to a half-empty bottle of cheap rum and two cans of Pepsi.

The woman nodded in Mayhew's direction, then glanced at the drinks. She lit a cigarette with an overly long wooden match as Mayhew tried to be nonchalant about staring at her hands.

"Do you remember me?" he said.

She did not look up. *"Como?"*

Mayhew pointed the camera at her and pretended to film, turning an imaginary crank like some idiot from a silent movie.

"Eso," she said, waving her finger, *"no se permite."*

"No, I've *already* filmed you. You don't remember? Over in Getsemaní."

"Como?" He could see the impatience rising to her eyes.

"Sus manos." He held out his hands, pointed to the palm of one, then the other. *"Sus manos. Sangrar."*

She screwed up her face. *"Sangrar?"*

"And your feet. I got it all on video. They were bleeding." He pointed at the tops of his own feet. *"Las heridas."*

Her eyes flashed and widened, and her face grew stony. She picked up a cellphone and began to dial.

"No, no, it's OK."

She was glaring at him as he took one of the beers and twisted the top free.

"See?" he said, grinning. "It's fine. I don't want to break the rules."

Still holding the cellphone, she tapped her watch twice with one of her long fingernails. Mayhew nodded and stepped forward. He took a long slug from the beer. In one coherent motion, she rose and stepped out of her shorts, hung them from the arm of the chair. She brushed past without looking at him, and he watched her, the way she moved, like any other woman, her hips rolling, all the way to a narrow bed against a wall on the far side of the room. She'd removed her t-shirt and was holding her bra. Above where she sat on the bed hung a torn poster of a circular stained-glass window. Mayhew hadn't moved. Without finishing the first beer, he opened another bottle. He'd not been with a woman other than his wife in almost two decades. He'd forgotten the ones before her. The thought both thrilled and saddened him, an old elemental shame come back like a lost melody or a ghost. The old script. With him no different from the rest, connected that way. It occurred to him how every woman he fantasized about was, at least in part, his wife, how monogamous he'd always been to his core. He'd not even seen another woman's bare breasts in ages, not in the flesh, except for one time in San Francisco when his hotel room window looked down into the apartment of a woman in her seventies, and he'd watched her undress standing in the middle of her kitchen, then wept to himself at the sight of her ruined breasts, connected beyond all explanation or reason to her aloneness.

He took another sip of Aguila beer.

The woman lay back with her elbow crooked out to her side, her palm cupped behind her head. She looked down awkwardly at the dark irregular nipples of her breasts as though they were something apart from her. Her hipbones, her belly soft between them, her thighs. Mayhew approached and knelt beside the bed. As she watched him, vacantly, her ribcage rose and fell. He could see the pulse flaring in her neck. "Please," he said. "Just—" He lifted her free hand in his, turned it over to examine the palm, then turned it back as she tensed up. She took a long breath, held it for a moment. Then she pulled free and rolled to face the wall. "Please," he said again. He didn't know what he wanted. She looked at him over her shoulder, in her eyes a trace of anxiety that sickened him. Finally, she eased back toward him.

"I just want to—"

When she offered her hand, he took it again in both of his, and began gently thumbing the palm. No matter how hard he concentrated, there were no scars nor any indication that the flesh had been parted or even bruised. But wounds that appeared miraculously could disappear the same way. Wasn't that the logic of miracles? He raised the palm to his lips, felt it stiffen as he probed the crevices there with the tip of his tongue, tasted salt, predictably, then the scent of jasmine or was he imagining that the way he'd imagined his tongue as the nail itself, and he rolled it now into a point and made as though to drive it with some force into the hollow of her palm. With this she pulled her hand away roughly. She shook her head and tapped her bulky watch again and shrugged. Mayhew ran his own palm over the curve her hip, watched the flesh goose-pimple over in the wake of his touch.

Now the man was knocking on the half-open door and already in the room, and the woman was sitting up on the bed working her arms into her bra.

"Have you seen the clock?" the man asked, his wrist thrust forward. "Time, time."

Outside, he and Mayhew navigated the dark streets back to where they'd met. "You had a good time?" the man asked. "You don't look like you had a good time."

Mayhew stopped him to look into his puffy face, the swollen inner corners of his eyelids. "Did the boy tell you anything about what I'm after?"

"I *know* what you're after," he said, his eyebrows raised. "How are you any different?"

"He said nothing about what I showed him?"

"I don't know that boy." The man squinted at his watch; he adjusted the metal wristband. "I don't want to know what you showed him. I don't care what you showed him."

"I have these video clips."

"Did she let you?" the man asked, tapping the camera. "It's her choice. But you have to pay a little extra."

"No, the clips I have are from before." Mayhew realized he didn't know exactly how long it had been since he'd taken them. "Back when we were shooting her over in Getsemaní."

"Shooting?" A look of suspicion finally registered in the man's face. "So you know her?"

"Yes!" Mayhew took a breath. "That's what I was trying to tell you before. I'm down here on assignment. Do you know about the stigmata?"

The man shrugged and straightened the long sleeves of his guayabera.

"The wounds of Christ?"

"You're confused."

Mayhew balled two fistfuls of the man's shirtfront and yanked him close. The guy was in his early sixties with a stringy, spent muscularity, a potbelly, and a mustache darker than his hair. "She was preaching over in Getsemaní. I'm not a fucking idiot. I've been looking at the video for weeks, and that's the same woman. I couldn't be more sure of it." But he wasn't sure. He wasn't sure of anything.

The man had gone limp. "Let go of me," he said gently. It seemed like an invitation. He seemed to be extending to Mayhew the courtesy of one last chance, but only when he began blowing a toy whistle he'd pulled from his pocket did Mayhew thrust him away. The man's face seeming to break open to issue a stream of Spanish invective the force of which sent Mayhew himself reeling backward. He turned to run, but as in a dream the street had come alive with silent men rushing in at him from all points. They were quickly upon him, jerking him here and there by the collar, tearing buttons from his shirt, the scent of sweet tobacco itself dealing blows. They kicked his thighs and shins, jabbed something dull and wooden into his chest and ribs, pushed him to the cobbles, stomped his hands flat against the angle of curb, the stink of the gutter frank and brutal now as Mayhew tried to *button up*, the phrase forcing its way into his mind like a mantra, his one memory of a failed football tryout decades before: *Button up, Mayhew, button up!*

They lifted him to his feet to watch him teeter, then set him on his way with a kick in the ass, laughing and cursing elegantly as he staggered. His pants were streaked wet, his shirt loose and open to the navel. He tried to laugh off having pissed himself, or to thank them for making him feel so welcome in his adopted city, but his tongue lost its way somewhere between the impulse and the act, catching on the sharp edges of his shattered teeth. He was drooling blood onto his sandals. There was pain everywhere, but only the pain in his both palms seemed to rhyme. It went back and forth, back and forth, in a language he'd only just realized he was fluent in.

"Hey," one of them called, a lithe guy about his size in a narrow-brimmed straw hat. He had Mayhew's camera. *"¡Mire esto!"* He raised it above his head with both hands, like someone about to slaughter a shin-high animal or drive a stake with a sledgehammer. He brought it down on the edge of the curb with enough momentum to shatter it, vastly. Another guy, the only native of the city Mayhew had ever seen in shorts, gathered up the pieces still attached to the strap and walked over to Mayhew holding them aloft with two fingers like something limp and disgusting. Mayhew slipped his arm into the strap as if nothing had happened, and staggered backward. Into the blast of their laughter, he offered up a curt salute.

It was late. In his delirium he thought he'd check the café again for Ruy, maybe get the skinny on what he'd seen earlier. What had they asked Ruy about him? Did Ruy have anything to tell? Could they have found out where he lived? But he shuffled along the streets for hours, trying to orient himself via the directions of the wall, running his hands along its rough surface, following its angles, and scraping his soles on cobblestones while waiters paused in their stacking of plastic chairs to watch him stagger past. When he finally turned onto his street, the curlews had been calling for hours. He answered them under his breath, his voice cracking in falsetto, then with more volume, laughing at their delighted replies.

The next morning he slept through mass and awoke in sheets haloed with blood and street grit. The door to his room stood open, a humid breeze filtering in. He rolled onto his ribs and tried to flex his hands. They felt bloated, his fingers stiff and fat. His right hand felt worse than his left, though the puncture in the palm of the left seemed to penetrate deeper. He held them up to the light. Was it a puncture? He slid from the bed to his knees and crawled to the bathroom, his hands balled in agony, then raised himself high enough to hit the light switch with his elbow. Fuck them. He would finish the job. He knocked his razor from the glass shelf above the sink, one of those stainless-steel contraptions in three pieces, not counting the actual razor blade, which he managed to dislodge only after a fifteen-minute struggle to hold it steady, finally taking the handle in his mouth and turning the head with the tender insides of his bent wrists. But then he couldn't pick the blade up off the floor. His fingers wouldn't work that way. He threatened them. He roared. He was close to tears. The phrase *fine-motor skills* came to him, but he couldn't remember where he'd heard it, maybe from his son's pediatrician. On the nightstand in a souvenir cup, he kept a dozen pens and mechanical pencils. He waddled the fifteen feet on his swollen knees and lifted himself like a satchel of bruised vegetables to sit on the edge of the bed. He lifted one of the pencils in his right hand, willing his fingers to close tight enough to hold it steady, then solved the problem by clamping it between his knees. Unsteadily, he lowered his left hand onto the metal tip as though over a flame, testing the edges of the gash already there, pushing down softly at first with the help of his right, then somewhat harder, as the burning sensation touched something deeper than he'd known, a bright clear pain that seemed to radiate up and into space like light through the back of his hand as he bore down even harder, rocking his palm slightly back and forth, as his sinuses cleared, his eyes stinging, and the congestion in his ears released itself with a pop, and he allowed himself to cry out with a rippling nearly joyful whimper, as, from beneath, the pencil's steel tip lifted the skin below his middle knuckle and his wrist like a tent pole under withered canvas; then it was wholly through, his entire body shaking with the cold and his breath ragged. He held this curious configuration up for inspection. Blood trickled freely now to his wrist and further down into the crook of his elbow. He turned it this way and that. He held it up to his nose. It was just before noon. He could hear the men working in the courtyard below.

He managed to lift the screen of the laptop and activate the icon of the editing application. There was blood on the beige curve of the mouse. He brought to life his favorite clip, the one in which the woman—he loved her, understood and forgave her reluctance to reveal herself to him—stands on the cable spool with her arms spread out before her, as though offering up some invisible bounty. There for the taking. He slowed the image in anticipation of the magical moment when she glances at him from the corner of her eye. Three other people hover in the frame: a middle-aged black woman in a gray housedress and wide wild eyes, an elderly man hunched next to her in a ragged sportscoat, and a taxi driver leaning on his arm as he watches from the lowered window of his cab—all looking at him with fascination and outrage. He nudged the clips forward, frame by frame. There. She's almost smiling. He lay back on the small bed, still damp with sweat and blood, and let himself drift, his body releasing into its pain, then sinking.

When he awoke, the boy stood over him. How long he'd been there, Mayhew had no way of knowing, but he was apprehensive about using his voice just yet, having surfaced from dreams in which it had been reduced to the simplicity and innocence of a curlew's call.

"*Mijo,*" the boy said, looking at Mayhew's pierced hand. It had only partially crusted over with blood; it oozed with each twitch.

"This is nothing," he managed, holding it up, smiling. The boy drifted backward toward the door. "It doesn't hurt that much."

"*Qué coño hiciste?*" the boy asked.

Mayhew struggled to sit up. "Do they know where I live?"

"*Quién?*"

"The people who were talking to my chess friend." He was ashamed not to know the man's real name. "Ruy Lopez."

The boy mouthed the words, then shook his head, shrugging. He seemed on the verge of flight.

"Did you see them? They're the people I used to work for."

"*Tengo algo.*" The boy held out a note that had been folded several times. "From her," he said, pointing at the frozen image on the computer screen.

His left hand still encumbered by the mechanical pencil half-way through his palm, Mayhew unfolded the note with difficulty. The boy started to help, but hesitated. There was no writing on the page, just the imprint of a hand in blackened blood. "What the hell is this?"

"From her."

"Jesus, what are you talking about? Who?"

The boy pointed again. "Her."

"No. I found her. You helped me. Thank you, but it can't be the same woman. Her hands are—there's nothing wrong with them. It can't be the same woman." He hated to hear how it sounded out in the objective universe.

The boy mimicked the act of holding the page up to be sniffed. Mayhew held the page up. He sniffed it. Mixed in with the machine-oil smell of blood he detected a trace of jasmine—not the real thing, perhaps, but what passes for jasmine among cheap perfumes.

"You're saying what? Go back? I can't go back there."

The boy seemed frightened anew by the amount of blood on the floor and the sheets and the nightstand. His eyes kept returning to the mechanical pencil. So Mayhew clasped it in his right hand as best he could and slowly drew it out. As the pain leapt to life again, he began to clench and shake. Now the boy was backing away in earnest, his eyes wide, his expression something new and more disturbing to Mayhew than the pain and the spectacle of his own pierced palm. When he'd pulled the pencil free, Mayhew smiled through his broken teeth. He clicked the lead-feeder mechanism twice and held it out bloody for the kid. "*Ayúdame.*" Mayhew offered his right hand. "Please."

The boy stepped forward to pull Mayhew to his feet. They moved toward the bathroom, Mayhew hobbling with his arm draped over the kid's shoulder. He reached in to turn on the shower but couldn't. The kid did it for him. There was blood on the yoke and shoulders of his t-shirt.

"You're not fucking with me, are you, with this handprint?" Mayhew asked. "It's not right to be fucking with such a loyal customer."

"Meet me tonight again."

"I don't know. In the same place as last time?"

"No. Do you need another camera?"

Fully clothed, Mayhew stepped into the shower stall, the water swirling around his broken feet like *vino tinto*. Later—it took a while—he managed to change his pants and torn shirt, which the boy later helped him rip into strips and wrap in loose bandages around his palms.

"OK. I'll be there," Mayhew said, finally. "When?"

"*Medianoche.*" The boy sat in the room's only chair, watching the clip. He rose to leave. "*Pero no en el mismo lugar.*"

"Where? What do you know?"

"Outside the church."

When the boy had left, Mayhew pulled on his sandals and limped down the stairs and three blocks to the telephone booth in the bodega. He bought some more rum but left it on the counter, the cashier wall-eyed, then dialed his home number, using the dregs of his memorized calling card, and waited for his wife to answer. His son picked up. Mayhew clicked the receiver down immediately. He lowered himself into the spot where Mark Twain usually sat and waited while the guy working the register tried to attend to an elderly woman with a long white braid, both of them fascinated by this *norteamericano* bleeding in the corner. The phone rang. Mayhew picked up. It was his wife.

"You sent them down after me?" he said, stunned by the normality that seemed to have engulfed him again, the brutal sameness, but not entirely trusting it.

"What would *you* do?"

"I'd let me finish what I started. I'd know how important it was to me. What I'd be willing to go through. I'd know what the man I'd lived with for fifteen years wanted."

"It's out of my hands, hon," she said. "Really." Her voice sounded unnatural, stilted, a performance for someone there with her. Someone other than their son.

"Got it."

"They're just worried about you. They showed up here. Was I not supposed to let them in?"

"Listen to me. You might be getting an email soon with a link."

"That would be nice." A faucet hissed briefly in the background. "In other news, I have a second interview at Sam's Club."

"What?"

"What do you think we're going to live on? Fuck yes."

"Can't you hold tight?"

"You've checked out. It's like I'm married to a fucking deadbeat. That's exactly what you are. You're no longer part of our lives."

"Don't say that." His left hand throbbed just out of sync with each thrust of his heart. Blood had soaked the linen bandages through. He turned so the cashier couldn't see it puddle and spatter on the wooden floor.

"It's the goddamn truth," she said. *"Hold tight?"*

"What's their concern? Why not just cut me loose?"

"Oh, I don't know," she said, her tone caustic as lye. *"What's their concern?"*

"I don't want them to—"

"What's *your* concern, huh? Clearly not me. Clearly not your son." Her voice grew muffled. "Mike, come here."

"No," he said. "Leave it. I'll hang up."

"Loser."

"That's nice."

"Fucking deadbeat. Going to whores down there."

A frost seemed to blossom in his bowels.

"Pathetic," she said. "Beyond the fucking pale. Unbelievable."

"Where did you get that shit?"

"You ready to tell me what the fuck you're—" She pulled herself up short, one of her well-worn rhetorical devices. "You know what? I don't care. I don't need you."

"I need you."

"Fuck. That."

He waited. "What's happened to your language? It's atrocious."

She fell to hissing and spitting again. He couldn't blame her.

"In front of Mike?" he said, but she didn't hear him. There were a number of shocks, thuds, and secondary crunching noises; he imagined the receiver coming apart, pieces scattering across the kitchen. Calmly he listened, as though from the next world. "One thing," he said. "Hey, hon, hon?"

The cashier had come out from behind the counter with a damp yellow sponge. Mayhew looked up. "Yeah, just a minute. I know—this is a problem, isn't it." He turned to the wall. "Hon, where did you get that 'whore' stuff? How do you know about that?" The cashier tapped him on the shoulder, handed him the sponge, and pointed to the spatter marks. "Yeah, I *got* it. *Lo siento.* I don't mean to be bleeding all over your store." Mayhew hung up. He lowered himself into an unsteady crouch. As he wiped, his sweat fell into pools of dilution in the blood. He used the front of the sponge, then the back, the sides. He was thorough. He rose with difficulty, head swimming, and hobbled to the cashier, who pointed at a trash barrel by the door.

"Oh, of course," Mayhew said, noticing more of his own blood on the receiver of a telephone in South America. But he was done cleaning.

He limped into the street, people glaring as they sidled past, and pointed himself toward the neighborhoods where he knew Ruy Lopez worked during the day. Ruy carried a beat-up wooden box with a cast-iron foot skid mounted on top and a hinged door on the side, and he always reeked of polish, his hands smeared with brown and black. The image of Jasmine and Bob conversing with Ruy—it worried him. His only comfort was that he could not decide if it had been real or not. That they'd come all the way down for a novice cameraman—and not a particularly good one—didn't make sense. He paused to lean on a bench at the edge of one of his favorite squares. Huge waxy banana leaves arched over a wrought-iron fence below a statue of some forgotten revolutionary standing in bronze next to his bronze horse. Mayhew wondered if it was hollow as he lowered himself to sit. The pain in his hands, his side, had taken on new sensation—fatigue—as though his wounds themselves were old and tired.

Ruy came to Mayhew as if summoned, his shoeshine box knocking against his thigh. He set up at Mayhew's feet without a word, lifted one of Mayhew's sandals onto the foot skid, removed a can of brown polish, and began to work the sandal straps. Ridiculous.

"Don't say anything," Ruy said. His voice was different, the Latin accent still audible, though muted; he seemed to have acquired a startling English fluency since last they'd spoken.

He looked up at Mayhew and shook his head. "Let me do the talking." For the first time in as long as he could remember, Mayhew began to worry about the veracity of his perceptive faculties.

"I'm taking a chance here." Ruy rubbed the polish into the straps with the bony middle fingers of each hand. The straps were suede so it didn't make much sense. "But we're all right for now."

"What are you? CIA? You were talking with my producer. When was it? Yesterday? What the hell was that about?"

Ruy smiled. "You're not looking too good, *viejo*. Those hands. See what can happen when you're out all hours of the night. You should get back to a regular schedule. You should spend some time with your wife and son. Maybe get back on your medication."

"Your concern's breaking my heart." Mayhew thrust his blood-black tongue through the gap in his top teeth. "I bet you're from Queens or Staten Island."

Ruy snorted. "Yank-ees suck," he chanted softly.

"Did you tell them about me?" Mayhew asked. "Where I live?"

Ruy looked up at Mayhew again from beneath his delicate brow. "How would I know that?" He drew a deep breath, then whipped a slip of paper from the back pocket of his polish-blackened jeans. Mayhew took it awkwardly with the two fingers commonly used to hold a cigarette. He felt elderly and arthritic. He had to bend forward, into a bristling pain around his right kidney, to read what was written there. An address with an apartment number written in green ink. Instructions. He hadn't heard of the street name before.

"You're going to have to trust me on this," said Ruy. "I know that's asking a lot, given the circumstances."

"Well, you never let me win at chess," Mayhew said. "I'll give you that much."

"I have my pride, my friend."

"So, with this—" Mayhew lifted the paper. "Do I have to eat it after it's memorized?"

Suddenly alert, Ruy lifted his head to take in their surroundings anew. In a moment, he was working on Mayhew's sandals again, smiling. "You're moving. Tonight. Bring everything you own. Everything single thing. We can't force you, but you'll do it. Because you're a good boy."

"What time tonight?" Mayhew asked. "See, because I have a date."

"I like you," Ruy said flatly. "Even though you're an asshole. It's a miracle you're not dead right now." He shook his head in mock wonder, his eyes wide. "I've never seen such an asshole as you. You have too much faith and not enough. How can that be?"

They both looked down at the mess Ruy had made of Mayhew's sandals and socks. Too much polish. "Jesus, I hope you're not expecting a tip."

"*Lo siento,*" Ruy said, mimicking Mayhew's gringo accent.

"You know about the girl?" Mayhew asked.

"Which one?"

"Oh, I don't know." Mayhew held up his bloody hands. "The one with a pair of these." Ruy looked at them blankly. There was blood in Mayhew's lap where his hands had been resting like doves. There was blood everywhere. This seemed to be Mayhew's new role: to bleed. It was hard to believe there was so much in him.

Ruy grew silent, pensive. "You're surprised that there's more than this world," he said, gesturing to the limestone wall, the shuddering banana leaves, the Caribbean sky. Mayhew saw the glint of the miraculous medal dangling thick as a silver dollar under Ruy's shirt. "There's only one who can see into them all, all the worlds, who can suffer the truth about them all. Only one." Ruy raised a thin finger. "And you're not him."

"That's obvious," said Mayhew. "Because I'm such an asshole."

Ruy stopped ministering to Mayhew's sandals. Mayhew had never been one for sustained eye contact, but he could now not look away from Ruy's face. As Ruy moved closer his eyes seemed overly large and dark brown and wet as aggies. He pointed at the paper on Mayhew's thigh. "Tonight."

"We'll see. I have to think about this."

"Have you given much thought to the terms of your visa?"

"What kind of a question is that?"

Ruy's leathery face went blank again and he closed his eyes in an expression of exasperated fatigue. He propped the heavy box on the bench next to Mayhew and sat down and opened the hinged side door. "See here?" Ruy held up something wrapped in soft black chamois and strips of rawhide. He paused to look at Mayhew with reverential silence, then began to untie and then unfold its leaves like some sacred offering. A pistol, heavy, steely dark, and oily. Mysterious indeed.

"Holy shit, how did I know it would come to this?" said Mayhew. Hadn't he dreamed the scene already? "Get it away from me."

"I'm not sure how much use it'll be, with your hands like that, but take it."

"Are you out of your mind?"

"See?" Ruy stood and raised his shirt and slipped the barrel into the waistband of his boxers. His ribs were like the downward slats of a broken ladder. "Like this." He let the shirt fall, draping everything.

"I'm an AV guy. I point a camera at what they tell me and hold it still."

"Well, you're *in it* now." Ruy removed the pistol from his pants, wrapped it again in chamois, and laid it with a precision akin to tenderness on the bench next to Mayhew.

"In what?" Mayhew tried to stand. "What am I in?"

"*En el mundo, viejo.* Deep." Ruy laughed silently. "You've been called out." Again, Ruy seemed to be picking up signals inaudible to all but himself; he suddenly seemed worried. "*Mira,* just take it. This isn't a movie. Do it for your old chess buddy." He laid the gun on Mayhew's thigh. Something about the gesture changed Mayhew's mind, and he was afraid to be alone.

"Don't make me come looking for you," Ruy said.

★ ★ ★

Back in his room Mayhew slipped the MacBook into his padded messenger bag and jerked the pistol from his waistband. It was still wrapped in chamois, and he slipped it in, too, then sorted out the empty water bottles from the few remaining full ones, the last two full pints of rum. Every movement echoed in his wounds, his every breath, as though the abrasions and punctures in his hands and chest were tasting the air. He began to strip the bed, but stopped. Bloody bed, he thought, missing man. And the tomb was empty. He left without shutting the door and seemed to move with the anonymity of the dead past the workman in the courtyard sweating as he grouted tile on his hands and knees, then out into the narrow streets, where he met the heat with resignation. For the first time, he took no notice.

At the cathedral, the afternoon service had begun. A dozen

congregants slumped in the forward pews, the usual ghosts, slow-moving and vacant, and he squeezed through the side door and padded past the first eight Stations of the Cross. He sat at the end of the pew directly across from the door to the little chapel where he'd often knelt before the Blessed Sacrament and listened to the priest fuss with his microphone. The man's fumbling rolled out like thunder among the arches overhead. Mayhew remembered the first time he'd received here. Arrayed in green, this same priest, having finished with the others, stood waiting at the end of the center aisle like some baleful archangel, annoyed with Mayhew for necessitating such pointless delay. Sit closer, *pendejo.* Nervously, Mayhew had approached. Having never put behind him his primary education at the hands of one last vestigial cartel of psychopathic nuns who drew their oxygen from the nineteenth century and warned against the act of chewing the host lest it flood his mouth with blood, never mind the unspeakable abomination of receiving while in a state of mortal sin, at the last moment, the wafer riding his tongue in the initial stages of salivary disintegration, he had resisted the urge to chew—or was it lockjaw?—and walked directly out, not into the usual blast furnace of tropical light but into a thunderstorm. He'd borne Christ along in the shelter of his mouth like some twisted Saint Christopher, then broke into a run to his building and up to the room, where he emptied the Tupperware of its contents—three half-eaten packages of saltines. Closed-mouthed, he'd washed and dried the receptacle, then lain the sticky host inside and sealed it off from the intrusions of atmosphere and time. A habit, this became, every morning, and with time the deposit of wafers had grown, like Christ's word in the heart of a convert—until his very real presence in the apartment had begun to weigh upon Mayhew. It soon occupied a space far greater than the volume suggested by the container in which it lay. He'd heard of people involved in similar shenanigans, the mind-fucked true believers and holy fools stuck at the threshold of the sacrament. It called to mind his own masturbatory practices, the sustained crescendo, the skill it required to delay pulling the trigger—surfing, he'd been deflated to discover it was called. (Must everything have a name?) Here again was the odd echo between sexual and religious practice, which perhaps was, at least in part, behind the Church's long-standing obsession with the particulars of erotic life—because practices by their nature were themselves so jealous when they did what they were meant to do: take root. And he never seemed more aware of the Real Presence of Jesus in his room than when he'd spend an afternoon religiously working through the continuously mounting, freely available gigabytes of amateur porn, the 10,000 sordid daily acts digitized and distributed by the participants themselves, as though to affirm some connection to the universal body. Mayhew had come to know it all as a yearning for ritual, forgiveness, and oblivion.

He would have to go back for the Tupperware. How could he have forgotten it? But the boy was sitting next to him now. The church was empty, the priest gone, and it was night.

"*Vayamos,*" the boy whispered. A tray of offertory candles wavered directly behind him, which must have been why the boy himself seemed to glimmer. Over the weeks, he'd provided Mayhew with several cartons of PowerBars, and though these had constituted 100 percent of Mayhew's diet, he couldn't remember the last one he'd eaten. The boy stacked a couple of the loose bars on the pew and slid them toward Mayhew with inexplicable discretion; the two of them were the only ones in the cathedral.

"I'm a little short on cash," Mayhew said. "Can I hit you back later?"

The boy nudged them closer to Mayhew. There was no question—Mayhew decided to take it in stride—the kid was glowing. With his cousin years before, he'd piloted a skiff out into the midnight waters of Buzzard's Bay, the sea black as glass, and with every stroke the oar had been limned in phosphorescence. The kid sitting next to him shone with that same luminescence—with its subtlety, if not its color. Or maybe it was a trick of the retina. That's why you learned to take these things in stride.

"*Vayamos.*"

"*Dónde?*" Mayhew asked. His hands were no longer bleeding, the palms crusted into claws.

Glimmering, the boy stood and lifted the backpack. He would have slipped his arms into the straps if Mayhew hadn't stopped him.

"Does this happen to you often?" Mayhew asked him, motioning to the soft light sublimating off the boy's shoulders like neon steam.

"*Como?*"

"Forget it."

He waited to make sure Mayhew had finished, then turned to genuflect. "OK. Follow me."

Mayhew did, the boy's outline drifting through the cathedral and out with him into the square, which was oddly dark now, even for night.

"*Hay no electricidad.*"

"Yeah, I can see that. Any idea why?" Mayhew asked. Maybe they could plug directly into the kid; he looked like he had energy to spare.

"*Sucede a veces.*"

"Before we get too far along—" By the kid's light, Mayhew fished the chamois out of the bag and unwrapped the pistol. He didn't know much about guns, other than that you operated them by pulling back on the trigger with your index finger and waiting for the loud noise and then you could put them down. "Not that I intend to use it, but you never know." He tucked it into his waistband in back, a stylish move he knew Ruy would appreciate.

"*Déjelo aquí.*" The kid's glow seemed to dim momentarily.

"Yeah, well, if I was all radiant like you, maybe I wouldn't need it, but I'm not, so I do." Mayhew glanced around at the dark square. "You saw what happened last time. I'm trusting you. Trust me."

"Do you want to see her?"

"That's what I figured this was all about—going back in there. Nothing happened that night, you know. I don't visit prostitutes. I'm not like that. Not that I'm—"

"But this time to see the real one."

"The one in the clip?" Mayhew pointed at the laptop in his messenger bag.

When the kid nodded, the glimmer smudged along the outlines of his form.

The door of a silver Benz sedan parked at the corner a hundred feet away opened; the interior light sparked to life, a pale yellow world in the surrounding dark. Mayhew would have thought it was a taxi. It wasn't. The driver, a woman, motioned them over.

"Is this our ride?"

He followed the kid to the car. When its bumper flared with the kid's reflected glow, Mayhew reasoned it couldn't only be in his mind, even though he knew such logic to be flawed. The boy held the front door for him. Mayhew slid in beside the woman. *"Que pasa?"* he said. The woman didn't respond; she was stone. With the boy in the car, she turned and snapped her fingers behind the front seat. The kid put something into her hand, and she thrust it out for Mayhew. A bag, empty, the size of football, and made of what appeared to be rough black silk. She seemed to consider its presentation explanation enough. Indeed, it was. Her hands were like something from the lower circle. Big and sinewy. Mayhew could imagine them on birds instead of talons.

"This your kid here?" he asked, jerking his head over this shoulder. "Or your grandkid, more likely?" It was getting ridiculous. The boy was filling up the car like one of those green light sticks. "He's a good kid. But have you noticed anything . . . special about him? Lately, I mean?"

She was much older than Mayhew had first thought. She seemed to be growing even older as they sat there. Larger, stonier. It was obvious she didn't think much of his sorry ass.

"You want me to—?" He pointed at the black bag and then at his head. Brilliant.

She sighed and shoved the black bag closer.

"En su cabeza," the kid said. "Now." Mayhew held the bag up to the light coming from the backseat. He slipped it over his head. As soon it was on, the kid whispered, *"Él tiene un arma."*

Mayhew felt the woman shift in her seat. *"Dónde esta?"* she hissed into his ear. He leaned forward and pulled the gun free from the back of his pants.

"Démelo."

He held it out in the direction of her voice. She snatched it away.

"I was getting around to handing it over." He heard her grunt, straining forward to slide the gun beneath her seat, where it rang up in the suspension coils. Then she jacked the transmission into gear, and the Benz jumped away from the curb.

At first he convinced himself he could maintain, for as long as necessary, a mental image of his position, his mind a vast Google Earth map in hybrid mode on which he moved like a pinprick of light. He would count off the turns, left, right, note the rise and fall of conversation at cafés, the hiss of other cars, their speed. He heard the whine of the zipper on his backpack. "You go ahead and help yourself back there."

Viciously, the woman hushed him. For a moment, he braced for a whack up the backside of his head. He felt the smoother surface of the highway now, the Benz having settled into fifth gear. Its front shocks needed work. He'd lost track of where he was, and he knew he'd soon lose all sense of time because he had never been good with it. Spending it. Saving it. Doing the things people did to mark its passage. He always seemed to waste it. All his life. Which would have been fine, he felt, maybe even in God's eyes, if he'd been otherwise enjoying it. He felt the car lose speed, veer right onto an exit. He smelled the diesel sloshing beneath him, heard the ticking of the directional. The sound of a tractor-trailer moving away, building momentum. The woman wheezing beside him. A right turn and a short stiff acceleration, the car jerking as if the woman's impatience were fueling it on. Behind him, the boy hummed a familiar tune; it could have been something by Shakira. The tires thumped down off the pavement. Now they were snapping and popping, the knock and scrape of tree branches closing in on both sides as right or left wheels dipped and rose, sometimes violently. Then the car was still, the engine off. The woman's door swung open, the kid's too. He heard them talking but he couldn't make out what they were saying. His door creaked open. The woman whispered, *"Sus manos."*

He turned in his seat and held them out as though for his mother's inspection after washing. Her fingers felt rough on his palms, the backs of his hands. He heard her wince and sigh. She thrust them away.

"*Vayamos,*" the kid said.

At either arm, they led him from the car. Bent forward, he shuffled like an old man, wincing under the jab of tree branches. He thought, At least my eyes are protected. The night was close and humid, and deep in the forest moisture dripped into the undergrowth. His feet crunched gravel.

They walked him across a threshold, pausing so he could step up and through another door, and the sound of the air changed as they seated him on a couch without much spring left in it. He felt fingers at the back of his head, probing for the edge of the black bag. It was gone. Mayhew wiped the sweat from his face and felt a blast of fear and panic. Across from him, in a wheelchair, sat the young woman, the one from the video clips, her hands wrapped in fresh gauze. On the pedals, her bare feet were wrapped as well. Not to have allowed him to prepare for such a moment struck him as profoundly unfair, even unkind. But how could one prepare? Hadn't he been preparing all this time?

She had yet to open her eyes, but he knew she was awake and this seemed to rouse the pain in his own wounds. They burned like rubbing alcohol, like liquid fire. At the same time it was a pain beyond the body.

The boy set the backpack on the couch next to Mayhew as the old woman lowered herself into a rocking chair and began to glide up and back, waiting. The boy no longer glowed; the radiance had become general, without a source point.

"I mean—" Mayhew began. The old woman clicked her tongue, shook her head. She whispered to the boy, and he jumped up as if suddenly remembering something and left the room. To Mayhew's right was a doorway hung with red curtains that parted slightly when disturbed by the oscillating fan. Each time they parted he could see with a little more detail what lay in the next room, where four or five men sat with their arms on a kitchen table. They wore the same black boots. In silence and without concern, it seemed, as to whether the curtains were parted or not, the men stared back at him. Every one.

He looked to the old woman. She shrugged slightly and fell to nodding her head, her eyes closed.

When the boy came back into the room, a box was balanced on his head, a new camera, of the same brand Mayhew had bought from him weeks before. He set the box down at Mayhew's feet and went off again and came back with a new tripod. Then the boy approached the girl bearing the wounds of Christ. He touched her wrist, and her head came up and her eyes seemed to surface in her face. She gazed across at Mayhew with the confusion of the prematurely awakened. That he had mistaken anyone else for this girl would be a shame he'd bear for the rest of his pathetic life. He was a clown. An idiot errand boy. The old woman clapped her hands and pointed to the equipment and made a little flourish with her index finger. The boy ran off yet again, came back with a plastic bag full of batteries.

Mayhew got busy setting up the camera. The old woman helped the girl to stand and two of the men in the other room appeared in the doorway and came forward to maneuver the chair closer to the couch. The girl lowered herself into it again. Mayhew pretended to be absorbed in the task at hand, but he was watching her as she leaned forward, her elbows on her knees. She began to remove the gauze from each hand, which coiled into a pile at her feet. Her skin was wan as the flesh of Christ in some seventeenth-century oil painting. And it occurred to Mayhew that this detail might explain a lot. He didn't know what. He didn't care. There was an aroma of open wounds and that of some flower he knew best not to name.

The camera mounted and in position, he looked around for a new place to sit, not so close to the girl. The old woman snapped her fingers again. She motioned for him to sit where he'd been sitting. He did. But the girl was wearing a tank top and a pair of blue terrycloth shorts, and he'd had dreams in which he'd confused her body with the bodies of wives whose husbands had videotaped them having sex with other men. He felt drenched in a filth that stung like salt in his wounds.

He stood again to reframe the video image of her hands, pressed the *record* button, and sat carefully back down. One of the soldiers from the other room came in with an open Bible—to which book or chapter, he couldn't tell. He took the Bible and thanked the man, and the man returned to the doorway, where all of the soldiers stood, the curtain finally parted for them all to see. Mayhew looked around at the circle of eyes. He tried to focus on the passage that had been marked in the Bible, but the girl slipped the book gingerly from his hands before he could read what had been indicated.

Now she took his left hand and opened the palm and, looking into his face, smoothed it gently as though clearing soot from a pane of glass. She probed the newly scabbed-over puncture and turned his hand to explore the exit wound, red and infected. The smell of hospital waste grew more intense, as did the smell of what he knew now to be jasmine. The boy leaned over as though having caught a whiff of the same and whispered, "*Olor de la santidad,*" then sniffed twice.

The girl began to weep silently. Before his eyes, she seemed to change into someone else, someone ancient. She raised her trembling hands for Mayhew to see, then offered her damp face to the camera. Above her hairline the blood began to well and spill into her eyes, along her chin, her palms and elbows and onto the floor. The old lady said something, and the boy positioned a bright-green plastic dinner plate where the blood thudded and splashed. Then he hastened to swab her face with a paper towel. The heat and smell overpowering now, Mayhew tried to edge back, and when the girl grabbed his right hand with her left he seemed to lose track of which belonged to whom. And when she set about separating his index finger from the rest, he tensed to struggle, but she held on tightly, and before his mind his body seemed to concede to what he knew she'd do.

"No," he whispered. "Too much."

The girl swallowed hard, but didn't speak. She didn't need to. Speech seemed superfluous and absurd. She glanced up at the camera once again, the blood on her face like runny mascara. Her grip grew even firmer and she succeeded in uncurling his index finger from the rest, and guided it to the dark blossom in the middle of her own right palm, and now he was in and fighting down a sob. He could feel the pulse of her heart in his fingertip. Mayhew looked around in disbelief at the soldiers in the doorway and the old woman and the boy.

* * *

He did not sleep, though during the return drive to the city he'd nodded out briefly and repeatedly beneath the black bag. In the darkness that surrounded him he half-listened to the rattle of the diesel engine and the old woman's prayers. She prayed as she drove, a voice without a body. Again and again he crossed the threshold of sleep, only to be jerked back by the occasional growl of a passing truck or the siren of an ambulance or, later, the cries of battling dogs. When the car stopped, he sat in silence and waited to be told what to do. He listened to air escape from the old woman's lungs as she groped for the pistol beneath her seat. *"Gracias,"* she whispered, closer than he'd thought, and nudged his shoulder with the handle of the gun.

"Oh," he said, his hand fumbling. "Thank you."

She thanked him again—the gruff warmth in her voice unmistakable now—and with the black bag still over his face, he pulled the door handle and got out. The old woman huffed around from the driver's side to leave something at his feet, then touched him again lightly on the shoulder with her big stony hands. He waited for the clatter of the diesel to fade into the watery ambience. When he finally removed the black bag, it was as though the city itself had been demolished and were in the process of being rebuilt. The sun hadn't risen, but the sky shone like light behind frosted glass. For the first time in his stay he felt a chill. Except for the wandering dogs, their eyes flashing from the alleys, the city seemed deserted. The chairs and tables had been stowed away; the curlews were silent. There was no moon. No one rushed up to him. He shouldered his messenger bag, painfully, and shuffled along a narrow street. The Lord had taken again to flickering in and out of existence, like a fluorescent lightbulb in an abandoned bodega, but then the same could be said for Mayhew himself. He had the most remarkable thoughts sometimes.

The main doors to the cathedral were locked. He doubled back and found the side entrance, a smaller door that he knew was always open, which seemed like a secret he shared with the creator of the universe. He slipped inside. He walked to the altar, up past the raised pulpit, to stand at the foot of the enormous cross, Jesus larger than life up there, though in the low ambient light Mayhew could see no higher than the weeping wound in his chest. He knelt to mumble a disconnected prayer, half plea, half boast. Then he rose to leave, but stopped to listen to the cavernous silence, the airless absence—it was the sound of suffering or of suffering newly abated or simply delayed. He traced the arch above one of the columns into the darkness. Someone had told him once that God was most Himself when he was silent.

Outside, the air had been changing, the city beginning to rematerialize. He followed the alley behind the church into a larger street, fingering in his pocket the paper Ruy had given him and repeating in his mind the address as if it were the Jesus Prayer. He located the street just blocks away, turned confidently into its narrow shadows, found the safehouse in the middle of the block. To his surprise, it was actually an apartment suite above a bar that featured techno music every night for wealthy tourists. Mayhew had stopped in once on one of his late-night walks to watch the men and women dance and to dream of a lost world absurd enough to include the possibility of his own participation in such practices. He moved through the empty barroom and across the sticky dance floor and climbed a set of carpeted stairs to a long hallway that stank of cigarettes. The note said he'd find the key taped to the back of an engraving, which he saw now saw was a Doré print of a winged being falling through starry darkness. The key was there and he used it to open the hallway's only door into a small apartment with a chair, an aluminum table, a dank kitchenette with a single window with thick panes that looked out onto a blackened limestone wall, dead ivy withering in the heat out there. If he ducked his head, he could see the angle of one of the cathedral's towers stenciled in black against the rising light.

He arranged his MacBook and camera on the tabletop and downloaded the clips he'd shot to the computer. He immediately opened them in his editing software and began to solve the problem of distilling the two and a half hours of footage into a single clip small enough to post online. Three minutes at most. He thought not to question the internet access. He worked quickly, silently, without noting the creep of light as the day evolved. He encountered none of the problems that had plagued him with the earlier footage. What he'd captured this time had been a performance, for him, a demonstration, a private audience featuring something as obscene as it was holy.

When he was finished, he posted the new version to his Vimeo account, then a copy on the ICBN blogsite under the heading "Still Convinced She's a Fraud? Behold." He searched his email history for one of Jasmine's company-wide HR announcements, hit *reply all,* cut and pasted a link to Vimeo, then hit *send.* He was all about redundancy. He even issued a Tweet to his seventy or so followers with the same link to the Vimeo post. He'd stripped the sound from the image, begun with an establishing shot of the woman in her wheelchair, cut to her wounds opening for the camera like rose petals in an old time-lapse sequence, the camera taking it all in with the silence and objectivity of the God he used to know. Initially, he'd worked to edit himself out of the clip—his finger in her wounds, his tears, the camera had seen it all—but then he gave in. To reveal his own presence as witness seemed important, to confirm that it had come from him. That he was the source— the mediator, the messenger. He watched the clip two or three more times before the first email announced itself with a dull peal in his mailbox.

That's when he heard a soft series of footfalls in the hallway.

He was suddenly aware of his physical hunger and of something else that, because he'd lost track of the time, he found difficult to frame and quantify. It was fear, he decided, finally, tinged with deathly nostalgia—because he knew his life might end this hour; maybe it already had. The lock engaged, the door opened, and there stood Ruy Lopez, thin as the crucified Christ.

"Hard at work," he said, swinging his shoeshine box into the room.

Mayhew had no answer other than to smile.

"You're a lot smarter than you look." Ruy placed a plastic bottle of Coke and a takeout order—a sandwich of some kind wrapped in butcher paper—on the table next to the Mac. "Didn't I say you'd come in to us?"

Mayhew just stared. The room smelled of roasted chicken and beans. From below, the thump of music began to rise. He realized he'd been hearing it for some time.

"Can I look?" Ruy asked.

Mayhew stood to make room. Ruy settled into the chair and waited for Mayhew to angle up the mouse and start the clip.

"No sound?" Ruy asked after a moment.

Mayhew shook his head, and Ruy fell silent himself. With the fresh appreciation of another's eyes, Mayhew watched him watch the clip: how it unfolded with a simple linearity. Simple was better. Always. Ruy drew a breath. There she is, her sallow skin, her narrow hands in her lap, her skeletal feet on the pedals of the wheelchair. Her hair is unwashed and she's limp. The camera is mounted, static. We see how the scene evolves, its inner logic, how the woman shifts forward with pain to sit across from Mayhew, how her hands reach out to lock his wrists. She's preventing him from rising. You can see he wants to leave. The blood wells and falls. It's clear that Mayhew's presence in the clip is part of the certification—for himself most of all. He could tell Ruy was weeping.

He remembered the Tupperware. He saw it back in his room, on top of the closet. "I have to leave." He could hear something different in his own voice. "I have to go back to my room, to take care of something."

Ruy glanced up, his eyes wet. "I wouldn't."

Mayhew's inbox signaled the arrival of another fresh email.

"No debate," he said. "I have to go."

"Do you still have the little gift I gave you? Your little friend?"

Mayhew raised the hem of his guayabera and turned to show the pistol tucked into his belt in the back. His pants hung from his bony hips. He'd lost thirty pounds. His own ribs reminded him of Ruy's.

"Has it come in handy?"

"I hope I won't have to use it. Will I?"

Ruy motioned to stand up. "I should come along."

Mayhew shook his head.

"Either way, I wouldn't bet against you." Ruy pointed at the screen, at the freeze-frame of Mayhew's hands in the woman's. "You are blessed."

"We'll see what the others think."

The eyes in Ruy's leathery face brightened. "What does that mean?"

"The clip's been posted. Just fifteen minutes ago." Mayhew would have gone into detail about where and why had Ruy not cut him off.

"Are you serious?" He leaned forward so that Mayhew could smell his breath. "Who told you to do that?"

"No one *told* me to do it," said Mayhew. "Wasn't it part of the plan?"

"What plan?" Ruy asked. Mayhew's inbox sounded again, then again. "Your plan? Who do you think set this all up? The visit. The internet connection. The safehouse?"

"Whoever you work for." Mayhew tried to loosen his shoulders, tried to smile.

"And who is that?

The music from below grew louder, the bass of the house beat rattling the silverware in the kitchen drawers like bones. "We're on the same side, right?"

"Forget about sides. You have no idea what you're talking about. What does an asshole like you know about sides?"

"You're right," he said, surprised by the anger in his throat.

Ruy snagged him brutally by the wrist and pulled him closer. Mayhew could feel his adrenalin rising, along with a small voice that told him to go easy, not to struggle. Ruy let go. "Have you always been such a child?" he asked.

All the way down the stairs, Mayhew could hear the Mac's inbox sound off again and again, with the frequency of falling rain.

★ ★ ★

Out in the street it was nearly dark. Mayhew walked with urgency but without clear direction, this way and that, now joining a group of blond German tourists, now following two local restaurant workers going home for the evening, now turning into a long street overhung with filigreed balconies and draping bougainvillea that reached almost to the cobbles. He circled toward his empty room through a series of cobbled squares, at the edges of which he moved along as unobtrusively as he could. He no longer stood out as an American tourist; the thought registered with a blow of pride and sorrow. It didn't take much effort to lose Ruy in the city's labyrinth. He took streets randomly, walking halfway along the block before doubling back. At the foot of the street on which he'd lived on for months, the old man who usually sat inside the bodega watching people use the telephone now leaned against the storefront. He monitored Mayhew's approach without affect, the only difference in his demeanor the movement of his eyes. And as he passed, Mayhew heard the man whisper, "Your wife called." But he made no other indication that he had recognized Mayhew or that he had even spoken.

Mayhew jerked to a stop. "My wife?"

The man nodded slowly, his eyebrows white and wild in the dark.

"What did she say?"

"She didn't," the man whispered, staring past Mayhew. "*Nada.*"

Mayhew drifted back along the curbstone, suddenly afraid again. They must be watching. But what could they do now? What power did they have over him? He wandered a ways up his street, then started back to the old man, thinking for a moment to send him in for the Tupperware, to pay him to retrieve it. But this was ridiculous. He stood staring at the old man, not know what he expected him to say.

The sheets in the room hadn't been changed. The air hung miasmic and cloying. It was still there, its slate-blue plastic lid visible just above the top edge of the closet. He felt certain someone had been there—the space vibrated differently. His body was like an instrument attuned to the physics of abomination. He dragged a chair to the closet, stepped up unsteadily. Even then he couldn't reach the Tupperware. In the closet he found a hanger, bent and worried it into a hooked arm, his wounds cracking and weeping under the pressure of the wire, and he stepped up again to jerk the container forward. Disturbed, it began to glow pale green. He lowered it to open on the bed. What was inside seemed to pulse now, cycling through waves of intensifications, cessations, as he peeled back the cover. The hosts had partially congealed, still moist and clumped, having taken the shape of one corner of the container. With exposure to the air, they began to deepen in color. The odor struck him as a mixture of festering saliva, such as one might encounter at the bottom of a toothbrush holder, and the piney aroma of furniture polish. He knelt. Gazing into the mass, he felt himself on the verge of tears. He thought he'd be ill, but this apprehension passed; and because he hadn't eaten for so long, he believed with each mouthful he swallowed that he might trace the physical and chemical processes of absorption into his blood and lymph, the pale green radioactivity spreading to surge through the leaky wounds at his extremities. When he was finished, he stood to look into the bathroom mirror. Was he seeing right? The impulse to fetch his camera passed like a wave; he didn't know where it was anyway. On the wall of the bathroom, the strange winged insects were still drawing a line from the floor straight up to a crack in the ceiling. When he moved his hand closer, they parted, circling to rejoin above the green glare on the plaster. He returned to the Tupperware—communion over—and after swabbing his fingers along the corner of the container, he licked the moisture from them, then toweled out the interior with a paper napkin and wrapped that napkin within another and put them into his shirt pocket. He started out into the street.

Afraid of no one—not even God.

The day had advanced—it was already gone. There was no one about, the streets empty. Finally, the city was his. As he walked, the light seeped from beneath his clothes, shining in spoked rays from his wounds. Wherever he looked, the radiance tracked his gaze, flooding with pale green the upper reaches of the dark colonial facades and the shuttered bodegas and the shadowed recesses. Soon he began to notice presences. Faces. They were stacked atop one another in an endless frieze of wide eyes and silent open mouths, poised as though in mid-scream. Why wouldn't this city be full of them? The crushing history of them peering from every crevice? His soul certainly was. With just their eyes they followed his passage, called forth into the realm of visibility, then falling back into darkness as he moved on. The mouths weren't open with terror, it seemed to Mayhew, so much as in wonder—and just as he recalled Ruy's words about seeing into all of the worlds, the light's intensity around him seemed to brighten.

He began to worry it would all go to waste, and he yearned for a witness to his radiance other than the faces floating in the murk, though he drew comfort in the knowledge that whatever they were saying, these silent mouths, was true. He had no time for anything less. As he roamed deeper into the night, it wasn't long before the wandering dogs came forth, drooling and corporeal, to whimper and to lick his wounds. Only the call of the curlews, their song beautiful beyond description, convinced him to sleep.

ACKNOWLEDGMENTS

Stories in this collection have appeared in the *Alaska Quarterly Review*, *Grain*, *Letters*, *Meridian*, the *Massachusetts Review*, and *Witness*.

This collection's long journey to publication was made easier by a number of people, in particular, Mark Powell, Emily Wojcik, Jim Hicks, Ronald Spatz, and the faculty, staff, and students of Spalding University's School of Creative and Professional Writing, who read or heard these stories at various points in their evolution. My most profound thanks, however, go to Ashley Alliano, without whose encouragement, patience, and love the collection would not have completed its journey into the light.

JUNIPER
JUNIPER PRIZE FOR FICTION

This volume is the twentieth recipient
of the Juniper Prize for Fiction,
established in 2004 by the
University of Massachusetts Press
in collaboration with the
UMass Amherst MFA Program
for Poets and Writers, to be
presented annually for an outstanding
work of literary fiction. Like its sister award,
the Juniper Prize for Poetry established
in 1976, the prize is named in honor
of Robert Francis (1901–1987),
who lived for many years at
Fort Juniper, Amherst, Massachusetts.